SQUAD GOALS

SQUAD GOALS

ERIKA J. KENDRICK

LB

LITTLE, BROWN AND COMPANY

New York Boston

Little, Brown and Company
Hachette Book Group
1290 Avenue of the Americas, New York, NY 10104
Visit us at LBYR.com

First Edition: April 2021

Little, Brown and Company is a division of Hachette Book Group, Inc. The Little, Brown name and logo are trademarks of Hachette Book Group, Inc.

The publisher is not responsible for websites (or their content) that are not owned by the publisher.

Library of Congress Cataloging-in-Publication Data
Names: Kendrick, Erika J., author.
Title: Squad goals / Erika J. Kendrick.
Description: First edition. | New York : Little, Brown and Company, 2021. | Audience: Ages 8–12. | Summary: Twelve-year-old Magic Pointdexter comes from a long line of cheerleaders, but to follow in their footsteps, Magic must survive summer camp Planet Pom-Poms, audition for a spot on the HoneyBee cheer squad, and steer clear of swoon-worthy Dallas Chase.
Identifiers: LCCN 2020017847 (print) | LCCN 2020017848 (ebook) | ISBN 9780316427142 (paperback) | ISBN 9780316427135 (ebook) | ISBN 9780316427159 (ebook other)
Subjects: CYAC: Cheerleading—Fiction. | Camps—Fiction. | African Americans—Fiction.
Classification: LCC PZ7.1.K476 Sq 2021 (print) | LCC PZ7.1.K476 (ebook) | DDC [Fic]—dc23
LC record available at https://lccn.loc.gov/2020017847

ISBNs: 978-0-316-42714-2 (pbk.), 978-0-316-42713-5 (ebook)

Printed in the United States of America

LSC-C

Printing 1, 2021

To my father, my Papa, who always
saw the Magic in me, even when
I didn't. Thank you for teaching
me love. I will spend my life
paying it forward.

CHAPTER 1

I've never wanted ANYthing more than I wanted this.

"Ready?!" a spirited voice peps from the middle of the gymnasium court.

I'm slouched behind the bleachers, gawking at the shiny Valentine Middle School HoneyBee cheerleaders, who are posted on all four sides of the oversized bee in the middle of the floor.

That's when the crowd yells back, "Oooh-kay!"

Then two Honeys speed-somersault across the gymnasium in front of a triangular formation of pink-and-gold girls. I watch the first Honey launch into a toe touch and follow that up with a high pike. Then the girl behind her hits the exact same jump and then the girl behind *her*. And when they come up for air, the crowd is on their feet chanting with them:

**From the East
To the West
The HoneyBees, we are the best.**

See, the HoneyBees, well, they're perfection. In the natural order of things, they're at the tippy-top of the human pyramid. And Gia Carlyle is their queen bee.

Seventh-grade super captain of the Valentine Middle School cheerleading team, Gia shakes her sparkly pompoms from center court, hitting every sharp motion with precision. I glance down at my unlaced, muddy sneakers. I can barely walk in a straight line.

**We're gonna B-E-A-T beat 'em
B-U-S-T bust 'em
Beat 'em, bust 'em
That's our custom
HoneyBees will readjust 'em.**

While the girls power-flip around the court, hitting four transitions and level changes, I shove a Twix into my

mouth and suck most of the chocolate from my fingertips. The leftover crunchy caramel gooeyness ends up on
my faded Valentine Middle tee.

When I look up, the squad has launched into a stacked
pyramid with a tiny flyer at the top holding her leg in the
air, high above her head. Then she lowers it and shoots
into a toe-touch basket toss way over the net. It feels like
she's soaring for two forevers while everyone is screaming:

Be aggressive
B-E aggressive
B-E-A-G-G-R-E-S-S-I-V-E!

One HoneyBee runs toward the crowd and cartwheels into a front twisty flip and intentionally lands on
her butt. Within seconds, the other girls follow. As they
land, they thrust their arms into the air and form three
rows of high Vs. They mean *business* as they shout:

T-A-K-E-D-O-W-N
HoneyBees, we want a takedown
HoneyBees, we wanna win!

The crowd is roaring so loud it feels like the whole
gymnasium is shaking.

"Another round of applause for our district cheer champions!" Coach Cassidy screams into the microphone. She stands in front of the Honeys with her bangs bouncing over her forehead. "Thank you, again, for coming out to the Valentine Middle Exhibition Rally. With just one week left in the school year, it's time to make those big summer plans. So if you'll be starting sixth, seventh, or eighth grade in the fall, we'd definitely love for you to join us for summer camp! For those of you who are thinking about signing up for Planet Pom-Poms, registration is now open in front of the locker rooms."

My eyes follow her French-manicured nails. It is now or never. I'd been counting down the years, months, and days leading up to this very moment. And now it's time to write my name on that registration form.

It was the only way.

At our school, girls went to cheer camp to become HoneyBees; it was a rite of passage. And now it's my turn. My turn to have a magical summer and stand in formation, shiny and bubbly, dancing to the perfect Honey-Bee beat. Even though making the team seems like the opposite of possible, I'm depending on three weeks of camp and a little bit of divine intervention to help me make it happen.

Coach gives us the rundown for the next three weeks.

4

"And we're looking forward to our amazing signature summer camp events that I'm sure you've all been buzzing about: the Pom-Pom Bonfire, the HoneyBee Carnival—and, as usual, cuts will be made after performances at the big MidSummer Family Brunch and then again at the HoneyBee Friends and Family Finale."

Coach's head hyper-spins around the gymnasium, causing her perfect pony to frizz. The hip-hop song starts and she dazzles the crowd with a megawatt smile. "We hope to see you all there!"

I'm now standing in front of the bleachers, right next to the registration table, watching Coach as she walks past me. I take a deep breath and muster the nerve to make this big declaration. "I'd like to sign up for camp," I say to Coach Cassidy's back.

"Well, hi, Magic," she says, turning around with confusion written all over her face. "I didn't know you wanted to be a HoneyBee. I thought you were coding or skating or…or something." Coach points her finger at my mouth. It takes a few seconds before I get the hint and follow her pointy nails to the chocolate stuck to my chin.

"Coach," I say, swiping at my chin with the bottom of my tee. "This is the year that all the Poindexter girls join the HoneyBees. I've twelve years old," I proclaim, "and now it's my turn."

Even though I don't fit the typical HoneyBee image, I've always dreamed of having my picture taken holding my prized pom-poms, just like all the other glammy girls in my family. And they've always said it was in my DNA. Buried deep in my DNA, maybe, but still there—somewhere.

It's no secret that I'm the granddaughter of the first Black HoneyBee to ever hit the floor. And to add to that piece of Valentine trivia, I'm also the daughter of one of the most celebrated Valentine alumni homecoming couples: a Los Angeles Lakers Hall of Famer and his equally beloved former Laker Girl wife. And now, my fabulously flawless big sister, Fortune, is "The Face" of the über-hawt Lakers cheer squad. This season, she's even on the supersized jumbo billboard at the corner of Sunset and Vine.

"So, no pressure," said no one EVER!

"Well, Magic, we'd love to have you," Coach says, sliding the registration form in front of me.

I take a deep breath and scribble my name on the line under five other middle schoolers. It's official; I'm going to camp. *And so is Cappie*, I think as I scribble my favorite—and only—friend's name, too.

"What's happening here?" My best friend's voice startles me.

I stumble over myself when I turn around. Capricorn Reese, my gorgeous, semi-famous best friend, snatches the paper from me.

"I'm going to camp."

She dangles the Planet Pom-Poms summer registration form in front of me. "And why is *my* name written under yours?"

I try to flash her my most charming smile. "Because you are, too?"

"As if!" She twists her CoverGirl features into a sour face. "Not now. Not ever."

I reach for my inhaler. "But—"

"Magic, are you nuts?!"

I try to snatch the form back from her.

"I don't want to be a cheer chicken, that's your thing." Her vintage motorcycle jacket hangs over her I DON'T CARE gray cropped tee.

"But, Cappie. I need you. And it's only for three weeks." I press my hands together and beg. "You can be my secret weapon. You've watched them a million times, so you already know all the dance moves. And you can help me learn the signature cheers and stunts. You were made for this. And, well…" I glance down at my untied shoelaces and stained shirt. "I wasn't."

See, Cappie was an admired dancer even when she

was just a tiny fetus in her mother's belly. By age six, she could dance circles around any Disney darling. Plus she's sizzly hot, and not just in a California bombshelly way (more like an anywhere in the galaxy kind of way). And she's mysterious with this razor-sharp edge. She did a Gerber's commercial when she was five, and the word around kindergarten had been that she drove *herself* to set. Insiders swore they spotted her wearing combat boots, leather riding gloves, and a temporary python tattoo. At six years old! And ever since, everyone wanted a piece of her. Even the HoneyBees. But no matter how much the Honeys tried to recruit her, she wanted nothing to do with them. She was *my* best friend.

"They're posers," she'd say every time the HoneyBees buzzed through the halls of Valentine. But she was smitten with the Laker Girls. "Now, *they're* legit."

I rest my hand on Cappie's shoulder. "Are you really going to leave me to fight off the KillerBees alone?" I nod at Gia and her co-captain, Yves Lopez. They're lethal, but Cappie, she's dangerous—and well respected. Me? Not so much.

Cappie rolls her eyes at me. "You know I planned on catching waves this summer." She was becoming an epic surfer and was already being watched by some of the elite junior pro-surfing teams.

Some people look up to Jesus, but Cappie is my shero.

"But I need you more than the waves do," I beg again. "I really want to give this a shot, even if I don't make it. You know it's always been my dream." I look her straight in the eyes. "Plus I want to make the Poindexters proud."

She studies my face as I mouth *Pretty please* at her.

"You probably want this cheer chicken crap more than anyone in here." My head bobs up and down as she looks around the packed gymnasium filled with Honey-Bee WannaBees. After studying my sad face, she throws her arm over my shoulder and grins.

"Does this—mean—" I stammer.

"You do know those girls are champions, right? That's who you're going up against."

"I'll work really hard, Cappie. I want to be a champion, too."

"What am I getting myself into? You're going to owe me big-time. But I guess since you've wanted this your whole life," she says, sliding the registration form across the table and turning to the crowd. "And yeah, you're definitely going to need some reinforcements with all this competition."

I follow her gaze through the thick crowd and stop when my eyes land on Dallas Chase, Boy Wonder. I sigh. Loudly.

"And bonus," Cappie snarks, patting down my undisciplined, wiry curls. "*He'll* be there, too. Boy Wonderful."

"Boy WONDER," I correct her, trying to look away. But no such luck. I'm staring right along with Cappie and the rest of the gymnasium.

It's no secret. Dallas Chase is a living legend and the rock star football quarterback for Valentine Middle. Rumor was that he moved here when his parents divorced two years ago from somewhere sophisticated, like New York City. Manhattan is still the best guess. But no one really knows for sure. He's the definition of cool. The town papers bragged that he's set to be the next star quarterback to step onto Valentine High's football field. Big colleges are already lining up to sit on the sidelines. He has his own entourage, and sometimes camera crews even follow him around.

"Magic!" I hear echoes of Cappie's voice, but I can only focus on Dallas Chase, boy of many talents—including making girls, old ladies, and even animals faint. Once upon a time, he looked at me and I swear I almost forgot my name.

"MAGIC!" Cappie startles me.

"Huh?"

That's when Gia runs over and loops her arm through

Dallas's. Oh yeah, did I mention that she's already got her eye on him?

"I think I'm going to be sick," I say, watching her snuggle up to him in front of everyone.

"And I think you're a smitten kitten."

"Ew! He's a boy and that's just...well, that's just perfectly gross." But my eyeballs are glued to the head cheerleader and the football star anyway. And I have no stinking idea why.

I'm gagging and simultaneously trying to decide which is shinier, Gia's honey-blond, highlighted hair, the bubblegum pom-poms she's holding, or her All-American toothy smile. In slow motion, she flings her head back into Dallas's arms and shakes out her Goldilocks mane. *Ick*.

Everyone knows that Gia has her claws in Dallas. I'd even seen their pictures online at some glittery charity gala for Habitat for Humanity. He was wearing a fancy black tuxedo with a junior ambassador pin under his left collar. And she was trying to hold his hand. *Double ick!*

"And just think, you'll get to see that all summer."

My eyes bug out of my head even more. "Dallas is going to be at Planet Pom-Poms?"

"Yep. He'll be right across the field for football camp."

"Doesn't matter to me. He doesn't even know I'm alive," I declare.

I sulk when I see Gia prance around center court, spinning over the giant HoneyBee wings painted on the hardwood floor. Yves power-twirls with Sammie, their third wheel. The rest of the squad gets in formation and they begin the dazzling sideline chant that they always perform right before halftime. The crowd is under their spell. I stand on my tippy-toes to get a better look. They are epic!

A tiny seventh grader popcorns through the air as the squad yells, "HoneyBees!"

The gymnasium explodes into applause and Gia and Yves begin one of the routines with wild stunts, crazy jumps, and a series of kicks that whiz way behind their ears. It's at that very moment that I start to shrink into myself and question my sanity. What was I thinking, signing up for camp?

"I can barely touch my toes," I mutter to Cappie.

"That's why you're—I mean *we're*—going to camp. Gotta start somewhere." She exhales and squeezes my hand.

"But they're sooo amazing," I sulk, feeling defeated. "I don't know how I'm even going to make it past first cuts at MidSummer."

She winks at me and mimics the team's dance steps.

"Like you said, with a few secret weapons." She knows every dizzying move; she can do it all in her sleep. "Basic stuff," she huffs.

I sigh and spin around—right into *him*. Dallas Chase, Boy Wonder. And right now, at this very moment, he's watching me watch him.

"You going to camp?" He shoves his prized hands into his black-and-gold football jacket.

Cappie makes a silly face behind his head and forces me to giggle. She always knows what to say or do so that life makes sense. And she was right, with her by my side—and maybe a summer miracle—I could be the next shiny HoneyBee.

"Yeah," I say, matter-of-fact. "I am."

"Cool," he says, and turns to walk away. "See you at camp, Magic Olive Poindexter."

That's my name. That's my *exact* name. And he *knows* it. He knows who I am.

He climbs the bleachers to join his friends but stops to turn back around and smile. I glance over my shoulder to see who's on the receiving end of it. But there's no one there. Just me. I try to move but I can't feel my legs. I can't even make myself smile back.

Cappie throws her arm over my shoulder. "Looks like he knows you're alive after all."

The HoneyBees spin around and take their final bows. And I still can't feel my legs. But I'm not the only one stuck. Gia isn't bowing. Or spinning. Or moving. In fact, she's glaring, directly at us.

Cappie leans into my side and draws an imaginary triangle between Dallas, Gia, and me. "Well, Magic, it looks like our summer just got interesting."

CHAPTER 2

"MA-GIC!"

"MA-GIC!"

The imaginary crowd explodes around me in my pink-and-gold bedroom as I continue to five-six-seven-eight through the signature Valentine Middle School HoneyBees cheer routine. My toes are pointed (*sorta!*) and my arms are almost straight. My left foot chases my right one through a grapevine and preps for the perfectly timed double pirouette. As I shuffle my feet around my room, the faces of my make-believe fans on all my posters mush together.

You got this, I reassure myself, and spot-check the

plastic basketball net that's hanging from the back of my door. I step onto the ball of my right foot and pull myself around into a turn. But instead of a coordinated spin, my legs involuntarily wobble from side to side.

Uh-oh.

My arms flail around in the air.

Ugh.

I'm twirling at high speed and I can't seem to regain control of my limbs.

Yikes!

As soon as I lose eye contact with the basket, I get super dizzy—my body scrambles for balance but it's already too late. I can't feel my feet anymore and I crash into the oversized mirror against the wall.

And then the worst thing happens: The mirror shatters into a zillion pieces.

Mom rushes into the room screaming, "Ohmahgawd, Pooh! Are you okay?"

When I pry my eyes open, she's leaning over me, raking her rainbow-bright nails through my uncontrollable mousy-brown curls.

"Perfect." I bury my head under my arms. "Seven more years of bad luck."

"Were you trying to do the double pirouette into a leap-jump again?"

"Into the splits," I explain, lying facedown on the floor. I can smell her perfume.

"Right, right," she says, nodding. "The signature routine."

"More like my very bad attempt at it."

"Did you forget to pull up from your core and spot?"

"Mommm." Massive exhale.

I peek from under my arm and eyeball my middle drawer. As she rubs my face like I'm a poodle, I reach for the drawer and pull out an open bag of Twizzlers from one of my not-so-secret stashes.

"Pooh."

I shake a licorice stick at her. "Comfort food is essential at a time like this."

She shoots me an encouraging look. "Don't worry, you'll learn how to master this at cheer camp. And by the way, I'm so proud of you for signing up last week. You'll have those turns, leaps, and splits perfected by the end of the summer."

I try burying my head deeper into my armpit. But that doesn't work; I can still feel her watching me.

I chew into the licorice.

My mom doesn't get me. No one in this family gets me. If I didn't know better, I'd swear I was adopted. But whenever I start going down that road, Mom whips out the picture of my legendary grandmother, Hattie Mae Jones.

"Genes are tricky, Pooh," she always says. "But you're the spitting image of your Grammy Mae." And like clockwork, she points out all the similarities. "Just look at that freckled nose. Those high cheekbones. And those bushy brows."

"And that wild, fluffy hair," I say before she does. My eyes roll around in my head and I mimic her. "You two could be twins."

"Seriously, Pooh. You could. Legend has it that Grammy Mae was a very special lady who had super-special gifts. And so far, you're just like her in every way." Then Mom pinches my cheeks and makes googly eyes at me.

I crawl around the floor and pull myself onto the bed. My one-armed teddy bear, Barkley, is the only one who truly understands my pain. My sister, Fortune, comes in a close second. But I always wish I could be more like her twin. She's perfect. She never needs an inhaler. Hasn't worn braces a day in her life. She's long. Lean. And luscious. And she's in her second year of being a professional cheerleader. She even just made captain of the Laker Girls. *Captain!*

I swallow a big ball of licorice and try to explain my

dire circumstance to my mom, who still gets mistaken for being my *other* older sister instead of my mother.

"Mom, you don't get it. You shook your pom-poms as a Laker Girl, just like Fortune. You can't possibly understand what I'm going through. I'm not built for this! How am I ever going to make the team?" I stand up, grab a shirt from the edge of my bed, and try tugging the *Adventure Time* tee over my belly button. It doesn't budge. On cue, Mom ties a sweater around my uncooperative pudge.

"It's clear that I'm not the cheerleading type," I say, fighting an epic battle with my denim button fly. I flash my eyeballs at the ceiling. "No, I'm more of the quintessential dark-artist type." I nod back at Barkley. "Or maybe I'm the coding, geekster-girl type."

Okay, so I'm still trying to figure out this whole "Who am I?" thing. But I have no rhythm, two left feet, and zero sense of cool. So let's just say the perky, peppy cheerleader thing probably isn't me—no matter how much I always wanted it to be. But when I look down at Finn's supersized head on my shirt, I don't know how it'll ever be possible.

"Your legacy is what you are, Pooh. You're a Poindexter, and we were born to cheer. Don't get discouraged. You got this, you'll see." Mom snuggles into my neck.

"Besides, there's nothing dark about my Pooh Bear," she says, sitting on the bed beside Barkley and me. "And we're so proud of you for joining the coding club. Just like we were proud of you for joining the pie-eating club, and the juggling club, and the hair-braiding club."

"And the cooking club, too," Dad pipes in as he passes my bedroom door with his head buried in his iPad.

"Thanks...I guess."

"Even though you didn't stick with any of them for more than a week." Mom glances at me and forces a smile. "Still proud."

Her eyes have that same look in them they did that one time Principal Pootie suspended me for starting a teeny-weeny kitchen fire in the cafeteria when I was trying to make Hot Pockets. After Mom negotiated with him, he lifted the suspension. But the ban on me being in the cooking club—and within fifty feet of the cafeteria kitchen—well, that one stuck.

"You're going to be a HoneyBee, too, Pooh. Just like the rest of the girls in the family. You just have to believe." She bats her long thick lashes. I bet that's what wore Principal Pootie down.

"But how do you know?"

Mom takes a deep breath and turns to leave the room. "I think it's time."

"Time for what?"

"Be right back," she says, and disappears down the hall. I fall onto my pillow and hear the Twix cookie bar hidden there break in half right under my head.

Mom dances into the room wearing a proud smile and holding a threadbare pink-and-gold bag in her arms. "These are for you."

"What's this?" I ask, hopping up from the bed.

I pad over to her and inspect the bag. VALENTINE MIDDLE HONEYBEES is written across one side in a faded cursive script. Mom opens the bag and pulls out a pair of big fluffy pink-and-gold pom-poms.

"These were your Grammy Mae's."

I gasp. *"Her* pom-poms?"

Mom places the poms in my hands and says, "She made sure we kept them just for you. There's no one else she wanted to have them."

Grammy Mae is an icon in our family, the wise matriarch of the Poindexter clan. But to me, she was even larger than life, my real superhero.

She had a way of always making me feel like I was the only person in the world when I was with her, even if the entire room was filled with people. I felt like I mattered, especially when I started school and my classmates made fun of me because I still had what Mom called "baby fat." Plus I wasn't into the latest fashions, and sometimes I needed an inhaler. Talk about uncool!

But Grammy always said she could relate. Then she'd sit me down and we'd drink tea while she told me one funny story after another about her struggles in school. She was teased, too, even though she never needed an inhaler and she wore the clothes her big cousins passed down to her, which sounded pretty cool to me. She explained that she was bullied mainly because she was the only Black girl in her class and the other kids didn't understand that being different didn't mean she didn't belong, it just meant that her story of moving to Los Angeles from Mississippi looked a lot different from the kids who grew up here.

Grammy was always so proud of her upbringing; she'd tell me the funniest tales about growing up in the South in a tiny town with only one market, one bank, and one ice cream shop. We'd snuggle under one of the quilts she made and talk over warm apple pie, which she'd always have ready whenever I visited. We grew even closer when I started to realize that I didn't look like anyone else in my family. They were athletic and played sports year-round. And even though Grammy Mae was round with chubby cheeks like me, she still played sports, too. She beat every girl that challenged her, and even some of the boys. And when she decided to become a Valentine Middle cheerleader, that's when she won all of her classmates over.

I look at the poms, wishing Grammy were by my side with a cozy quilt and a slice of her delicious apple pie. "What am I supposed to do with them? Do you think I'll be able to use them at camp? They don't look like the shiny poms the HoneyBees use. They're huge . . . and old."

"Not old, Pooh. They're vintage," Mom corrects me, placing her hand over mine. "She told us to make sure you got them and kept them close." Mom shrugs and rubs my cheek. "These are very special poms, Pooh," Mom says. "And now they're yours."

"But," I say, pushing them away. "I'm not a HoneyBee."

"But you will be. Soon."

"How can you be so sure? You just walked in on me sprawled across the floor. You remember that, right? Five minutes ago?" I nod at the shattered mirror glass on the floor. "Seven whole years!"

"Not according to Grammy Mae. You're twelve now. You're right on schedule to make the squad. This summer is going to be yours." She holds the poms under my chin so I can get a good look at them. And I can't help but exhale into a smile that matches Mom's.

"They smell just like her."

"We've kept them in this bag for all these years. Just for you."

"It's almost like she's still here. If I close my eyes, I can see her."

When Grammy Mae died last year, my heart broke into tiny pieces. She never judged me—not even when I chopped my hair off in a desperate attempt to look like Fortune. She told me I was still beautiful while she took pictures of me and my new haircut. And when I came home from school, I discovered that she'd put them on display all around her room.

"I really miss her, Mom."

"I know you do, Pooh. You two had a very special relationship." Mom snuggles me close and touches the poms gently. "Move the streamers to the side and look at the handles. See what they say?"

And right there, I see Grammy Hattie Mae Poindexter's initials stitched in gold thread around the cloth band: HMJ.

My eyes go wide. "This is so amazing. Her initials before she was a Poindexter."

Mom kisses my cheek, and I fall back onto the bed again. This time I smush a Twizzler into my mouth. "So," I say, smacking on the candy. "These are supposed to be what? Like...magic?"

"They're special, Pooh. Just like you." She rubs my

hair and stares into my bugged eyes. "And they connect you to your Grammy Mae. So, yeah, in that way, they *are* magic."

The streamers catch a few sparkles in the light, and my heart skips a beat. I pick them up and hold them to my chest, inhaling the scent of Grammy Mae's perfume. My heart starts to pound as my chest swells. Mom called these pom-poms special, magical, like me. Maybe she was right. If I didn't know better, I'd swear Grammy Mae was right here, sitting next to me.

And then I sigh, because that's exactly where I'd want her to be.

CHAPTER 3

My big sister, Fortune, is everything! She's the most epic nineteen-year-old in the whole world. And she's all mine. I'm lucky because she doesn't mind when I stand in the doorway of her room and watch her perfect her makeup. Sitting at her white-and-gold vanity, she looks like an oversized doll. And her room is the coolest. It's all grown-up with furry pillows and a matching shaggy rug at the foot of her bed. She even got permission from Mom and Dad to paint it a lemony color with white-and-raspberry trim.

"Well, good morning," Fortune sings, causing me to

stir from my perch in her doorway. "It's your big day! The first day of camp!"

I force a tight smile and shrug, pretending that I'm cool with the scariest day of my life unfolding right before my eyes.

"How's my fave little sissy doing?"

"I'm your *only* little sissy." I giggle, padding into her room. She always says that, like she's got a million other little sisters stashed in her giant walk-in closet somewhere.

She gets up from her vanity and runs over to me, knocking me onto her fuzzy rug and slobbering me with kisses that quickly turn to tickles.

"Fortune, I can't breathe!" And I really can't—I'm laughing too hard to catch my breath.

"Say it! Say it and I'll stop," she demands, laughing almost as hard as me.

"Okay, okay! I'm your fave little sissy."

"And?"

"And God was having a good day when he made me."

"There. That wasn't so bad." She hops up and pulls me with her. "Now, come sit with me." And then she plops down onto the big raspberry chair in her room, snuggled into a spot right under her huge window. I call it the sunset window because if you sit there at the exact right time, you can see the sun setting behind the long row of bushes in our backyard. The best times are when she invites me to sip hot chocolate and watch the day slip into night right before our eyes.

She tosses a pillow onto the floor and taps the chair. "You've been standing in that doorway for ten minutes. A girl's obviously got something on her mind. I know I'd be covered in feels if it was me going to camp for the first time ever."

I look down at my hands and study them. "It's just that I'm not so sure I can pull this off. I'm not like the rest of you."

"But that's the exciting part. Being different doesn't have to be scary. This is the summer that your whole life is going to change. And it's going to be amazing."

"Then why am I so nervous?"

"It's a lot to take in. But you won't be alone. You've got Cappie. And—"

"But that's it," I say in a big rush. "I don't know anyone at camp besides Cappie. I mean, I've seen some of the girls around school, but it's not like I'm friends with any of them."

"You're going to make so many new friends. Girls who are talking to their big sisters right now and feeling the exact same way you do."

I stare out her window at the tree with the nest of baby robins in it. I don't want to tell her that the thought of making new friends is a little scary, too.

"I really want to make the team and be just like you guys. I want to make you proud." I eye the chocolate stains on my shirt. "But look at me."

"Yes. Look at you. You're perfectly you. And that's all you need to be. You'll learn everything else over the next three weeks. That's why you go to camp, Sissy—to learn."

When I shrug, she pulls me closer. "You're going to get to do all my favorite things this summer. You're going to go to the Pom-Pom Bonfire and then there's the HoneyBee Carnival. And MidSummer and Finale are tons of fun, too."

"But that's when they make cuts."

"True. But it's also really cool and super fancy. They turn the Great Lawn where they have all the practices into a beautiful outdoor ballroom with swanky tables and nice linen. And all the families get to dress up and come. So we'll be there to cheer you on," she says, throwing her arms into a high V. "And celebrate your victory."

"But what if I don't—"

"Listen, Sissy. You can do this. You only need one hundred points total. And you'll have two big chances to earn your points. They get that you're learning all this new stuff, so at MidSummer, you just gotta get fifty. And then at Finale—"

"But, Fortune, what if—"

She ignores me and keeps explaining with enough confidence for both of us. "It's mainly about three things: dance, stunts, and chants. And don't worry, Sissy. They teach you all of that. They teach you everything you need to know."

But my idea of hitting the dance floor looks like a bad version of the robot. How am I ever going to pull this off? Dance, stunts, chants...oh my! Grammy Mae's special poms couldn't have come at a more perfect time.

CHAPTER 4

"**M**agic, this bag isn't going to pack itself," Mom warns. "And your bus leaves in an hour," she reminds me, giving me that look that means serious business.

I watch the Poindexters scatter around my room, tossing stuff into my new suitcase with Supergirl plastered all over it. I chew on another Twizzler, still in shock that this is all happening—in one hour!

Fortune opens my middle drawer and spies an opened bag of Twizzlers. She tosses them into my wastebasket.

"You, of all people," I say as I smack down on my

comfort candy, "have no idea how terrifying the next three weeks are going to be for me."

"You're in for the summer of your life! You'll see," Fortune says, high-kicking her leg into the air. I watch her pointy foot whiz way past her ear and stop somewhere behind her head.

I hide my face under my pillow and only peek out when I hear Mom huff, "Get up and get working on this bag, Pooh."

"Guys, I was thinking. Maybe I made a mistake believing I could do this. It might not be too late to sign up for coding camp instead."

"You can do coding camp next month if you want," Dad says, studying the school website on his iPad. "It says slots are still open. So it'll be there for you after cheer camp."

I smush the pillow deeper into my face.

"You can do this, Champ," Dad rallies like he always does whenever I have one of Mr. Bower's big science tests at school.

I poke my head out from under the pillow and watch Dad eye Mom, who nods back in agreement. "I completely understand why you're getting cold feet right now. It's a big deal to have to go to a new place with lots of people you don't know and do something you've never done before. But you're *my* Champ. And nothing is too big for you to handle."

Dad was always so positive and sure of himself. He played for the LA Lakers and was a real champion, plain and simple. He's been on top ever since he was twelve and shot the winning basket for his Junior Olympics basketball team. His Valentine jersey is even framed in our hallway outside of Principal Pootie's office.

"But I'm not like you, Dad."

"Exactly. You're like you." He eases the pillow from my clutches and looks at me with fire in his eyes. "And that's even better."

I grab the pillow back and roll into it.

"You gotta give yourself a fighting chance," he says. "What's our positive affirmation for the day?"

"I am fearless and brave," I mumble from inside the pillow. "I have nothing to be afraid of."

Dad pushes the pillow out of my reach. "Sit up, Champ. And say it like you mean it."

I spin around on my butt and my feet dangle over the side of my bed. "And my fears will not stand in the way of my goals."

"And what's your goal?"

"Dad! You know my goal." I strain my neck to look up at him.

He kneels beside me and squeezes my hand. "I know. But you gotta say it out loud. That's how we manifest our destiny."

I stand up in front of my family with my shoulders pushed back and my head held high.

"There she is." Dad beams.

"My goal is to attend Planet Pom-Poms Cheer Camp and become a HoneyBee."

Dad puts his big arm around me and lifts me off the floor. "That's my girl." And then Mom throws her arms around my waist and Fortune squeezes me from outside the Poindexter bear hug.

I sigh into the family huddle. "I'm really going to miss you guys."

"We'll be there for MidSummer, Sissy," Fortune pipes up. "Dressed to impress and ready to cheer you on."

"But that's two whole weeks away," I say, falling back onto my bed.

"Well, you might have a surprise visitor sooner than that." Fortune giggles, then winks at Mom. "When you least expect it."

Mom pushes my suitcase toward me. "Everything's going to work out, Pooh." She searches around my dresser until she finds the bag with Grammy Mae's poms buried under a blanket. "And don't forget these."

I take them into my hands, feeling warmth emanate from them. They sparkle in the light, and I feel tears prick my eyes. "I wish she was still here."

"She loved you more than anything in the world," Mom says, ruffling my hair. "And she'll be with you— every step of the way."

"I wish I could get one more hug from her. And hear her tell me it's all going to be okay."

Dad wipes an almost tear from his eye. "We all do."

"Don't cry, Dad."

"I'm fine. My eyes are just sweating."

"Let's do it for Grammy Mae," says Mom, putting her hand in the center of our semicircle. Then Dad puts his in, too, and Fortune follows suit.

"C'mon, Champ." Dad winks at me.

I toss my arm in with theirs and we all bounce up and down like every basketball team does before the big game.

"GOOO POINDEXTERS!" We giggle-yell in unison, our voices building to a thunderous roar right there in my bedroom.

"Gotta love those Poindexters!" a familiar voice yells from my bedroom door.

"Ohmahgawd!" I scream when I turn around and see Cappie strut right into my room and toss her military duffel onto my bed. "What're you doing here?"

"I called for reinforcements," Fortune fesses. "Mom was right; that suitcase wasn't going to pack itself."

"Cappie!" I throw my arms around her in a bear hug. "You didn't stand me up. I was so afraid you weren't going to come."

"Not a chance. I'm a girl who keeps her word. I'm all in for three nauseating weeks at Planet Pom-Poms." She turns to see that my suitcase is nearly empty. "Now, let's get you packed so we don't miss the big dumb banana bus. Making the squad and becoming one of those cheer chickens is still your big girl dream, right?"

Capricorn rages through my closet, and within minutes, my suitcase is at the door waiting.

"Thank you, Capp. I really don't know if I could get through this without you."

Fortune hangs next to my bed and crosses her feet at her ankles. "Cappie, you know we love you like you were one of us. Thank you for being the best BFF in Santa Monica."

Cappie lives next door to us. We met when I was learning to ride my tricycle and she was already doing tricks on her ten-speed. I always say Cappie should've been born into the Poindexter clan instead of me. But whenever I mention that, Mom just tells me that things turned out exactly the way they were supposed to.

"I couldn't have asked for a better Christopher Robin to my Pooh Bear," she'd say before grabbing my round cheeks and patting down my undisciplined hair. And then she'd blabber on about me not understanding until I had a daughter of my own someday. And I knew what she meant—sorta. The part about Cappie always being there for me was true. But the part about having a baby of my own someday...*ew*!

"Magic was right. She needs me more than the waves do this summer," Cappie explains to Fortune. "The ocean will still be there in three weeks, when camp is over."

"I'm surprised you're not driving the bus to camp yourself." Fortune pokes at Cappie.

"Touché, Fortune Teller. But after that last minor incident with Uncle Charlie's Porsche, I've been strongly advised to stay out of trouble with the parentals and with—"

"—the poe-poe?" Mom finishes. She giggles to herself and tosses me my favorite Girl Power concert tee.

"This time I think I've actually been given my final warning. Getting in trouble used to be cute, but I think that cuteness has officially worn off." She settles into the bed and her luscious, wavy Hollywood hair, one of her many industry calling cards, hangs down the arms of her motorcycle jacket. "I think they're actually over me this time."

"Your fingerprints have been on file since you were, like, three," Fortune adds.

"That's what happens when you steal cars and joyride up the Pacific Coast Highway, Capricorn," Dad jokes. "Eventually somebody's going to notice you can barely see over the steering wheel."

Ignoring my dad and my epic battle with my denim button fly, Capricorn pushes me out the bedroom door. But not before I grab a handful of Twizzlers from the trash and shove them into the pockets of my too-tight Levi's. Halfway down the hall, I reach around for one, but they're gone. Pockets empty. I grin at Cappie, the most genius pickpocket this side of Los Angeles County.

"You got everything, Pooh?" Mom asks as we step outside and head to the car.

I scan all my stuff.

Suitcase: check.

Sleeping bag: check.

And then I freeze.

"Be right back. Forgot something."

"Hurry. The bus leaves in twenty."

I race back into the house and jog up the stairs, two at a time. I fly down the long hallway and around the corner, right into my bedroom. I flip on the light and there they are, still on my dresser waiting for me.

Grammy Mae's poms.

I take a deep breath and pad over to them. Then I close my eyes and pull them from the bag. When I peek out of my left eye, I can see them, quietly twinkling back at me. "Okay, Grammy Mae," I say. "Let's do this!"

Grammy Mae's sweet scent circles around me. My fingers start to tingle and I can actually feel her, right here next to me. And I don't want to run. And I don't want to hide. And I don't want to be afraid.

"Hey, Champ," Dad yells from the bottom of the stairs. "It's time to go! You ready?"

He's right, it is time for camp. And I have no idea what the next three weeks of my life are going to be, but with Grammy Mae beside me, I think I'm finally ready.

CHAPTER 5

My eyeballs are fixated on the grooves in the rubber floor of the bus that's filled with WannaBees headed to Malibu for cheer camp. I scan for empty seats and swipe the sweat from my forehead. Cappie and I finally settle into the absolute last row at the back of the bus and I spin around to the window. A quick wave goodbye to the Poindexters, my showstopping sitcom family, and we're off to Planet Pom-Poms.

"Magic, are you absolutely sure about this?" Cappie asks, suddenly urgent. "Because I can pop that door open and we can be on the back of Uncle Charlie's Harley before lunch."

For a quick second, I wonder if she's going to kick down the emergency back door and make a run for it.

I glance at the bag with Grammy Mac's poms and then smile back at Cappie. "As sure as I'll ever be."

Cappie sticks her gum under the seat and stretches her strong legs into the aisle. "Oooh-kay." Then she pretzels herself into some sorta yoga pose. She hearts yoga. Says it makes her butt supreme for rocking the waves.

As the other WannaBees laugh, swap stories, and trade snacks, I scoot closer to Cappie. "I'm glad you're here with me." I reach for a Twizzler from one of my secret stashes in my bag and break it in half. I offer her one but she takes out a bag of kale chips instead. *Gross.*

"Where else would I be?" she says, starting our secret handshake we made up in the Reptile House at the zoo last year. We end it with a slinky body roll and a finger snap.

Cappie has always been my safe place. I fetch my sunnies and snuggle up beside her. I guess you could say I got lucky when God assigned besties. Within seconds, she's asleep. She can fall asleep anywhere, even at the zoo in the Reptile House. Which is exactly what she did after we made up our handshake.

I stare out the window at the plump trees dotting the Pacific Coast Highway. The blur of green leaves whizzes by, peekabooing the ocean, and the lull of the bus rocks me like a baby.

A short dream later, we pull behind a sea of other yellow buses in the parking lot of California University. Sunshine. Palm trees. Ocean breeze. And there they are—the Valentine Middle School HoneyBees. Sporting matching pink-and-gold uniforms with equally chipper pom-poms that sparkle in the sunshine, the HoneyBees are all perfect tens. Their hair hangs over their shoulders, rolling effortlessly into big, bouncy waves. I touch my own brittle curls and wince.

Gia and Yves stand in front of the other HoneyBees on the big campus lawn and make actual bumblebee noises.

"Buzzzzzz." Hands on hips.

"Buzzzzzz." Feet pressed together.

"Buzzzzzz." Bright white smiles on display. "Buzzz. Buzzz."

They're in perfect unison as they greet the newest fleet of WannaBees.

"You ready, Magic Poindexter?" Capricorn pokes at my rib cage.

"Guess so." I suck in a lot of air before taking a step forward.

Capricorn rubs my shoulder when my breathing

becomes noticeably spastic. "Your eyeballs. They're like jumbo saucers."

I try to act normal, but it's too late. When I spy Dallas Chase running to catch a football heading for our bus, normal goes straight out the banana window.

"Yep, still a total smitten kitten, I see." Cappie laughs. "Meow."

I fake-shove my finger down my throat and pretend to gag.

She shakes her head and reaches for my suitcase but I don't let go of Grammy's poms.

"I'll keep this."

"What's in there anyway?"

"My Grammy Mae's pom-poms."

"Why? They're going to give us HoneyBee poms for the summer."

"They're my lucky charm," I say defensively.

She shrugs and heads off the bus. "Okay, lovebird."

I follow her, trying to explain myself. "I'm nobody's lovebird." But I stop talking when Gia and Yves greet us as we exit the bus.

"And lookie here, it's Magic Olive Poindexter," Yves says nastily. "Also known as Tragic Magic."

I wobble down the second-to-last step on the bus. I'm focused, trying to dodge her venom, when I completely miss the last step. In slow motion, I fall forward. Face-first. I can see Yves's tiny feet take two giant steps backward right beside Grammy's pom bag.

An obnoxiously loud thud echoes behind my fall and everyone turns to look right at me and my face, which is now buried in the dirt. That's when I realize the lens in my sunglasses is starting to crack right down the middle, my arm is screaming at me, and there's the tiniest rip in the butt crack of my jeans.

"Welcome to Planet Pom-Poms, Poindexter," Gia says from somewhere over me.

"You were right, G. She's absolutely dork-tastic." Yves kicks the dirt off her signature white shoes, straight into my mouth. "And ultra tragic."

"Yes, she really is a total Tragic!" Gia declares, and bursts into a fit of giggles.

I don't dare move, except to spit out hunks of dirt and gravel. All I want is to click my sneaks three times and disappear, especially when I hear Dallas's voice inching closer. And closer. I try clicking my heels anyway. At this point, it can't hurt, right?

"You okay down there?" he asks from somewhere above me.

Sprawled on the ground like a moron, I look up and lock eyes with him, still stuck in the dirt with no idea what to do next until Cappie rescues me, pulling me back up to eye level. "You really know how to make an entrance."

I spy Coach Cassidy beelining to us. "Is everything okay over here? That was an ugly fall, Magic."

"I'm fine," I say, rubbing my arm. "It's just a little bruise." It does not feel little. It feels like my arm is on fire, but I'm not going to let anyone know that.

"If it starts to bother you, go see the nurse. She's at the infirmary."

"Okay, Coach." I fidget with my clothes before shooting her a thumbs-up as she heads toward another group of girls.

"And she wants to be a HoneyBee?" Yves gawk-points at my pink-and-white Fruit of the Loom undies that are hanging out right below my belly button.

"You all right?" Dallas asks. Again.

I inch my fingers toward Grammy's bag and slide it back to me. "I'm good. Supercool." Then I yank my Levi's over my panties. "Fan-fricking-tastic!"

"You sure about that?" he asks, touching the cherry-colored bruise on my arm. "You might want to get that checked out. The nurse's station is on this side of campus. I can show you if you want."

"NO!" Gia power-switches her hips over to us. "That won't be necessary. She's fine!"

No. I'm not. Not really. I hold my bruised arm with my good hand. *Not fine at all.*

"Right, Poindexter? You're totally fine." Gia digs her Beedazzled nails into my throbby skin and pushes me through the crowd, far away from Dallas. "There's nothing to see here. Get into two lines." When no one moves, she forcefully positions me with the other thirty Wanna-Bees and yells, "NOW!" Then she just glares at me. Hard.

"Tough crowd," Cappie says when everyone finally scatters.

"I think my bone shattered into a zillion pieces," I whisper-moan back at her, feeling the fiery pain shooting up and down my arm.

Dallas shakes his head and points at my arm before heading toward the football field. Then he waves. I have no idea what to do next. I can't be expected to remember how to wave back. Not at a time like this. But, then again, this is really basic stuff here.

"Poindexter!"

Uh-oh. Gia is not amused. But Cappie is. Her snorting confirms that she's majorly enjoying this sideshow. Gia storms down the line of WannaBees to the very end, stopping directly in front of me.

"What exactly do you think you're doing?" Her deep-pleated pink-and-gold mini blows over her butt to reveal her custom HoneyBee panties. And she doesn't bother to yank her skirt back down either. Instead, she breathes into my earlobe and the coconutty scent from her shampoo hovers in the air around us.

"We all know who your family is, Poindexter. And we don't care!" She steps back and her squinty eyes size me up again. "You think you're hot stuff because of your last name?"

"Uh. No." I fidget with my fingers. "No, I don't."

It was true that my family was basically famous, but I never shoved my genetics in anyone's face. And I didn't expect special treatment because of them either. I mean, seriously, it's not like I was actually carrying that special gene around anyway.

Gia pops her hip. "I had to work my butt off to get to where I am and if you think you're just going to walk onto *my* team, think again. I don't even know why you're here."

My eyes dart around her head and I try my best to hold back tears. But honestly, I don't know how much longer I can keep them hostage. This is all too much! Really, I *just* got off the bus.

"Well?" she challenges me. "Why *are* you here?"

I swallow. "Because I—I want to be a HoneyBee."

"But you can't dance. You can't flip. You can't stunt. You can't—"

"That's why she's here—to learn," Cappie fumes back at her. "Just like everyone else. Seriously?"

"Oh look," Gia huffs. "It's the ex-D-list star Kettle Corn."

"That's Capricorn to you."

Gia villain-laughs so hard she has to hold her stomach. "You two oddballs really think you're going to be crowned with the coveted pink and gold?" She turns to Cappie. "Once upon a time, Capricorn, we thought you were built for this life. But now we think you're just another weak WannaBee."

Gia snaps her fingers in the air and the HoneyBees swarm into position. When she turns her back, Cappie nudges me to shake it off and we break into our secret Reptile handshake. My body roll is awkward, mainly because my arm is on fire, but I don't care. This only makes us laugh harder, until Coach looks up from her clipboard.

Coach Cassidy could easily be mistaken for a Valentine High HoneyBee. This was her second year as the middle school coach and gossip around school made it sound like she was super nice.

"She gives her captains tons of freedom to lead the team," an in-the-know WannaBee buzzed in line. "Gia and Yves have been captains for two years. They'll be starting eighth grade, so it's their last year."

"Welcome, girls, to Planet Pom-Poms!" Coach announces from the front of the big Great Lawn while Gia spreads her arms into the wind and takes her reign over us. This is her turf, after all. The girl is a regular at Planet Pom-Poms; she's been coming since sixth grade. "We look forward to an incredible three weeks with you," Coach says.

"Three stomach-turning weeks," Cappie snuffles.

"Don't worry." I shrug. "I probably won't be here nearly that long."

"We are the reigning Santa Monica District Cheer Champions," Gia announces. "And we have every intention of taking the throne at Regionals next year." She looks around at the sea of WannaBees.

"And that's where you come in," Coach continues as she steps onto the stage with her clipboard in one hand and an iPad in the other. "We are a team made up of twenty Valentine Honeys; however, all the returning Bees have to audition again for their spots, except the captains, Gia and Yves. That leaves only eighteen cheer positions open for next season. And while we obviously want the slickest stunters and the best dancers, we are also looking for spirited girls to join our HoneyBee family."

Gia clears her throat and interrupts Coach. "But history has shown that only a select few actually have what it takes to thrive in the Valentine HoneyBee hive. It's an honor and a privilege." Then she takes a long moment to survey the lawn that's now bubbling over with anxiety and excitement. Clearly she does not think any of us are deserving of that honor and privilege.

"What does she know? I bet she can't even spell privilege," Cappie snarks back.

I snort-giggle loud enough to get Coach's attention. We try to pull ourselves together, but it's too late; we're all over Gia's radar again.

Coach Cassidy finishes explaining her expectations to us and we all listen so closely that you could hear a pom-pom drop. "We'll be sizing you up and measuring your endurance, your talent, and your potential. You'll learn our winning routines, our spirited chants, and our death-defying stunts. But this isn't for everyone and unfortunately, some of you will be sent home at MidSummer."

"Truth: Some of you need to get back on that bus right now." Gia mumbles under her breath, so low I can barely hear her.

"But, G, there are always a few WannaBees with a death wish," Yves snarks back.

My knees start to buckle at the thought of dying, but within seconds, my attention is captured and I'm stuck in a HoneyBee trance. The returning champion cheerleaders turn the Great Lawn into their very own circus as bouncy somersaults whiz up and down the field, and toe touches popcorn through the air. It's all razzle dazzle, a live pink-and-gold Planet Pom-Poms party. Even Cappie looks impressed.

Then she catches me watching her and turns her nose back up. "They're like...whatever."

"So," Coach says as she steps onto a pink-and-gold platform. The squad surrounds Gia, buzzing as they shake their glittery pom-poms. Two strong girls lift her into the air like a goddess and we all watch as she raises her arms in victory, looking down over her dynasty. Coach applauds the jaw-dropping Honeys. "Now, on behalf of the Valentine Middle HoneyBees, we welcome you!" Her voice echoes over all of the Great Lawn.

Then Gia peps, "To the hottest summer of your little lives."

I suck in all the air around me and realize I am utterly, *supremely* hypnotized.

CHAPTER 6

It's already been a long day and camp hasn't even officially started. We all got checked in at registration, took
a grand tour of the campus, and then headed to the café
for dinner. After dessert, we were assigned dorm rooms
and roommates. I picked Cappie and she picked me, so
that part was easy-peasy-lemon-squeezy.

Capricorn and I finally settle into our dorm room on
the west end of campus. I stop to watch the sunset from
our bay window while she flings my suitcase onto my bed
and insists that I get my arm checked out.

"It's turning blue," she says as she leaves to sign us up
for the dance and stunt workshops. "It looks like roadkill."

She is right. And now it feels like the bus rolled over it and left it for dead. So I decide to take the long walk across campus to see the nurse before the infirmary closes. When I get there, I poke my head into the small room reserved for the injured. Two boys are already waiting, so I scoot down a few seats away from them and try to ignore their fantasy football babble.

After a few minutes, I'm so lost in the poster about the universal sign for choking that I don't even hear my tummy grumble. Too bad the boys do. They stop talking and start looking at me. I look the other way and shove a Twizzler into my mouth and chew hard enough to drown them out. That's when Nurse Molly's door opens and Dallas Chase walks out—and heads right over to *me*.

"I guess you decided to check out that arm." He turns to the boys in the room and signals to them that he's fine. I watch them get up and head toward the door before he says, "That was a pretty gnarly fall you took off the bus."

As if I needed reminding. "It's not too bad. Hopefully."

"It's probably just a bad bruise or a small sprain at the worst," Dallas says, looking at my arm as if it is the most interesting thing he's ever seen. "But it's better to get it checked out and be on the safe side, ya know?" He watches me nod back at him. "Do you mind if I go in with you to see the nurse?"

My eyebrows shoot into my forehead. Why would he want to do that? He just finished seeing her.

"I'm sort of a physical therapy geek in training," he explains. "It would be cool to see what Nurse Molly says about this."

"Magic Poindexter," Nurse Molly calls, checking my name off a clipboard with a warm smile.

Dallas eyes me.

I shrug, but the butterflies in my belly don't allow me to actually speak. Dallas takes that as his cue to lead the way back to her office.

"So your name's really Magic?" he asks. "Like, it's your real name?"

"Uh-huh," I say as my palms get sticky. "Had it my whole life."

He looks over at me, and then he shrugs. "Cool."

I shrug back, mainly because my nerves won't let me find any other words for this moment except *Cool*.

I follow Dallas into Nurse Molly's office, looking around for more words. But when he looks back at me, I shrug. Again.

Ten minutes later, I'm back out into the cool night air . . . with Dallas. Nurse Molly warned me about putting too much pressure on my arm over the next few days. She wrapped it in a white bandage that I thought made me look wimpy.

"Good thing it's only a bad bruise," Dallas says.

"Yeah," I manage to mumble, still clueless about why Boy Wonder is even walking next to me, not to mention talking to me.

In the nurse's office he kept asking a zillion questions about the tendons, ligaments, and some other stuff that I could've cared less about. Then to my surprise, he followed me—all the way past the Great Lawn and into this massive meadow filled with oversized daffodils. He kept talking about ligaments and bone tissue, and I just tried not to freak out like I did the time I met the backup dancers for Girl Power, my absolute favorite band, and I couldn't stop rambling on and on about stupid stuff, like peanut butter.

"So why'd your folks name you Magic?" he asks when we get to the middle of the Daffodil Field. "Are you guys, like, new age hippies?"

"Hippies? No. I don't think so." I shuffle my feet, still not sure how to talk like a normal twelve-year-old. More than anything, I want to freak out.

"It's just that everyone knows who your dad is. And I definitely don't think of Sir Damon the Dunker as the hippie type. But your name—" He stops talking and looks over at me. "Magic is a really cool name and everything, but your dad, he's like a legend. He's in the Hall of Fame. They retired his jersey because he's *really* cool and—"

"I get it," I blurt, before I can catch myself. It was all finally starting to make sense:

1. Why he took such an interest in my bruised arm.
2. Why he didn't laugh when I nose-dived from the bus.
3. Why he's walking me back to my dorm, which, FYI, is in the *opposite* direction of the boys' dorm.

"Get what?" he asks, popping a piece of raspberry watermelon bubble gum into his mouth. He offers me one but I pretend not to notice.

"Nothing."

"Dude, don't do that. I hate when girls do that." His raspy voice cracks a little when he says it again. "What do you get?"

Now what was I supposed to say? Where was Cappie when I needed her? She'd just come out with it, take the bull by the horns and choke it to death.

I stop walking and work up the nerve to square off with him. As the daffodils swallow up my legs, he blows a big bubble. More than anything, I want to pop it. Instead, I push my wild curls over my shoulders and just go for it.

"The reason you're talking to me, why you've been so nice to me—it's because of my dad." My voice is shaky. "So, yeah, I totally get it now. He's supercool and I'm not, but whatever."

Dallas Chase doesn't say anything. He doesn't even blink.

"You want to meet him...or something?"

He raises an eyebrow. "Who wouldn't want to meet your dad? But what's that have to do with what I'm saying?"

"Well, why else would you be talking to me?" I lower my eyes. "It makes perfect sense now. My dad was an athlete, you're an athlete...." I'm so tragically *not* an athlete.

He shakes his head and grabs my good elbow to pull me back into our walk. "That's not why I'm talking to you."

"Then why are you being so nice to me?" I say, trying not to sound pathetic.

"I'm sorry you even have to ask," he says, nudging my shoulder. "You know what," he continues, unbothered, "you remind me of someone I used to know. Someone who wasn't exactly an athlete either, but eventually became one."

I believe him. Mostly because his eyes seem sincere. And Fortune always says the eyes are the windows to the soul. I don't stare long enough to see what his soul looks like because I realize that he's staring back. At me. And then I'm just standing there watching him watch me. And just when it starts to get really awkward...he smiles.

Decided: I'm definitely going to introduce him to my dad. And get him an autograph. Dad is always signing stuff for far less important people.

"You could be an athlete, too—if you wanted to."

"I do," I whisper. And when he doesn't say anything I press him. "What else do you think I'm doing here?"

He chuckles. "You sound like you're just going through the motions. Like you don't really believe you can become an athlete."

I look at him sideways and try to piece him together like a puzzle.

"Trust me, I get it. I come from a family of athletes, so everybody just knew I'd be some kind of athlete, too. Kind of like you."

We walk for a while without saying anything until I

break the silence. "I really do want to be a HoneyBee. It's all I've ever wanted."

"Why?"

"It's always been my dream. And maybe my grammy's. And okay...maybe I want to do it for my mom, too... and my sister...and my dad and..."

"And for you, too?"

"Well, yeah. Of course."

He pats me on the back. "Now you don't sound like a poser." Then Dallas Chase winks at me. "And if that's true, you've got a little work to do."

That's when I shift my hips around and a horrible thing happens—the rip in the back of my jeans tears straight across my left butt cheek. I pray he doesn't notice. "Okay, so maybe I do have some work to do."

Dallas starts walking again. I power-skip to catch up to him, covering the hole in my pants with the back of my hand. And he doesn't say a word about it. Instead he looks straight at me and smiles. "You know what you are?"

"I think the word you used was *poser*." Now I'm hanging on to his every word, like when Ms. Jennings, our homeroom teacher, called out the names of the students who got to go to lunch early on Fridays because they were model citizens all week. Only this was a little different. Ms. Jennings didn't make my mouth turn dry and my stomach queasy. Maybe I was allergic to Dallas Chase.

I squirm around the daffodils and shiver when the wind blows them against my legs.

"You've got everything you need inside of you already. It's what my football coach always tells me whenever I get down on myself."

That's when the wind spins around my neck and bolts down my spine. I shiver again. "But this is me. This is all there is," I say, stepping back so he can get the full picture.

"I'm talking about your potential. With some endurance work and focus on muscle-building, you'll get stronger in a few weeks. I see it every year at football camp." He eases his hands into his jeans and blows a big purplish bubble, even bigger this time. "Logan could barely run fast enough to catch the ball last summer and now he's the best receiver on the team. It just takes time and effort and dedication." Then he asks the dreaded question. "You ever work out?"

I grimace at the thought of running on the treadmill, getting nowhere—the exact opposite of how I hope the next three weeks of my life at cheer camp will go. "Other than dancing around in my room by myself and falling on my face? No, can't say that I do."

"Well, if you ever want to work out, I'd be down to train you." That's when he takes my phone out of my hand, punches in his number, and calls himself. Then he laughs when he says, "Now I've got Magic in my cell."

This is where I should probably tell him that Cappie's already promised to help me. But when she agreed to train me, Dallas—Boy Wonder—Chase wasn't in the picture. And now that he is, how am I supposed to say no?

He hands my phone back to me. "So just text if you want to go for it. I like to work out at night when everyone else is sleeping. And no one even has to know. I won't tell anyone if you don't want people to know that you're training."

A secret life with Dallas Chase? Is he serious?

I have to take a deep breath. "Can I ask you something? For real?"

"Shoot."

"Why do you want to help me?"

"I told you, you remind me of someone I used to know." And then I think his cheeks turn red when he smiles this time.

I smile back, and I surprise myself with how good I'm getting at it. "The girls' dorm isn't too far from here. And I don't want you to miss curfew. I can walk the rest of the way."

"Cool." He shrugs again, but this time when I shrug back no more words are needed. Except these:

"It was my grandmother," I say.

"What about her?" he asks, looking right at me.

"She was the one who named me Magic."

"Nice," he says, before taking a few steps backward. "She must have known you'd be special."

I watch him pull his phone from his back pocket. And within seconds, I hear my cell ding.

Dallas: Let's make Magic happen.

CHAPTER 7

I slip into the back of my dorm with a racy heart, clammy hands, and wobbly knees. When I hear the sound of footsteps getting closer, I round the corner and take the stairs, two at a time, straight toward my room, trying to escape being caught out after curfew. It's 9:12 PM and I'm hoping Cappie decided to call it an early night. My bedtime was normally nine thirty at home, but Cappie didn't have one. She hadn't had a bedtime since she was five. But maybe, just maybe, she was exhausted from all the excitement of the day and already passed out on her bunk bed.

"Magic Olive Poindexter."

Nope. Wide awake.

"Magic! Where have you been?"

For some reason, I don't want to fess to Cappie that I was just with Dallas Chase. Even though it was a total coincidence and completely innocent, something about sharing this epic secret makes my heart turn into a drum major and beat against my chest. Then my hands get sweaty and I don't want to touch anything. So I plop down on the bottom bunk to avoid looking at her.

"I went for a walk?" I say, rubbing my hands against the comforter until they're dry. A walk is not entirely a lie. I'm aware that it's not entirely the truth either.

Her head dangles from the top bunk. She eyes me suspiciously. "The infirmary is not far from the Great Lawn, just past the meadow with all those daffodils. I looked it up on the map." She unfolds a big map from our welcome packet. "See." She points to the red cross. "Infirmary."

I check out the map. Planet Pom-Poms is shaped like a big rectangle, with the girls' and boys' dorms on opposite ends of the rectangle and the gym and infirmary on the other two ends. There's a giant field in the middle of it all that is divided into six sections: the Great Lawn, and the cool Daffodil Field where you can lounge and chill.

But if you want to play sports, there is a tennis court, football field, sand volleyball court, and a running track that circles it all.

Cappie hops down from her bed, sniffing around my head. Her Spidey Senses are on alert. I try to focus on Barkley sitting on my pillow, but even he knows I'm lying.

"Magic Olive Poindexter!"

I try but I can't hold it in one second longer. So I scoot to the edge of the bed and confess, "I was with... Dallas—Boy Wonder—Chase."

"As in head KillerBee Gia Carlyle's crush?!" Cappie gasps. "As in your major crush, too?"

"I'm not crushing on him! That's just... just... no way! We were just talking."

"Then what's the deal with the bright red cheeks and the sweat beads around your brows?"

I swipe at my brows and try to shake off the red. But when I glance in the mirror, my entire face is still flushed. I shake my head. Now it's even redder. But that's my story and I'm sticking to it... even though I can't deny that he makes me feel like a hot cup of cocoa topped with squishy marshmallows, all caramel excitement and chocolate nerves.

"Cappie, you're making too big a deal out of this. It's nothing. Really. He just walked me back from Nurse Molly's."

"Alone?! At night?! Through the Daffodil Field?!" I'm starting to worry her eyes are going to pop out of her head, so I fall backward on my bed and just blurt it out.

"Okay. Okay. If you want to know the whole truth..." I eye Grammy Mae's poms that are watching me from the nightstand. "He said he wants to *train* me."

I splash through the entire story. And when I'm done, she's sprawled out on the floor, staring at the ceiling with her mouth wide open. "This is major!"

"I know, right!" I sigh.

A knock comes on the door and Coach pokes her head into our room. "Lights out in ten minutes, girls. Diagnostics are tomorrow. It'll be a long day."

We both nod. But as soon as the door closes, Cappie begins pacing around our room. Her arms are folded. She means business.

"This is serious stuff, Magic. Gia is with him. Or at least she thinks she is. And it could get really dangerous if she discovers you're secretly hanging out with him. You do want to survive the next three weeks at Planet Pom-Poms, right?"

"But—"

"Trust me, Magic. You just shouldn't see him again." She squares my shoulders and stares at my eyeballs. "This is for your own good. Those girls are ruthless. You're committing social suicide by even thinking about making moves on Dallas. The KillerBees will bully you until they destroy you, and you'll ruin your chances of becoming a cheer chicken."

She's walking fast and now I'm on her heels, following her around the room, trying to keep up. "But I'm not *seeing* him." I sigh. "He only wants to train me so I can get in shape and maybe work on my muscles to get really strong and—"

That's when Cappie presses her hand into her hip and sucks her teeth. "Isn't that why *I'm* here? To help you?"

"Whaddoyoumean?" I fake-ask, looking the other way.

"I'm a junior athlete, for crying out loud. And I gave up the first half of my summer to help you." Then she presses me harder. "Right?!"

See, this is where it gets kinda dicey. Yes, Cappie's right; she's supposed to be my secret weapon at cheer camp. And yes, I could work with her, step up my cheer game, and try to get fit. But the thing is, she can be so impatient and kinda mean whenever it takes me too long to learn stuff. Take the time I wanted to learn how to surf. After trying to help me catch a wave for two hours, Cappie just gave up and left me floating around the Pacific Ocean. When I finally schlepped back to shore, she wouldn't even look at me for forty-five minutes. We were on our fourth round of s'mores by the time she talked to me again.

And I've never told her how it makes me feel when she gets huffy with me. In her defense, I get that I'm a slower learner than, well, *everyone* when it comes to coordination. But it doesn't make me feel good when she just gives up on me.

"Yes, of course you're the one who's supposed to train me. Duh!"

"Then no more funny business with Dallas Chase," she says, studying my face. "I can't have you getting murdered by Gia over a boy. Pinkie swear?"

I shove my pinkie in her face. "Pinkie." But at the last second, I cross my fingers behind my back. Just in case. "Swear."

CHAPTER 8

The next day, the Great Lawn is filled with flying girls trying to out-stunt or out-tumble each other. The HoneyBees are in the front rows soaring through the air. Rows of pink-and-gold aerials flip around the lawn and before I can catch my breath, back handsprings are tumbling toward me. If I had to bet, I'd say some of these Bees were doing somersaults before they could crawl.

"Good morning, girls," Coach Cassidy announces from the stage in front of the Great Lawn. "Welcome to Diagnostic Day, also known as D-Day. We're so happy to have you here with us." She smiles over the group and claps for us. "Today we'll be dividing you into groups based on your skills."

The HoneyBees take their positions in front the WannaBees. Gia makes those annoying buzzing sounds with her mouth again and we all watch as the other Honeys join her.

"Yes, today will be a little long. And yes, it will be challenging for a lot of you, but all I ask is that you do your best and let your light shine through. I believe in you."

Gia pops her hip and the other HoneyBees pop their hips, too. Then she snaps her fingers and they all scatter across the lawn to tighten us into formations.

Cappie smirks at Gia and her Beedazzled entourage. "They're like her robots."

"We need Tragic Magic and Kettle Corn to pay attention!" Gia mutters to Cappie and me while two Honeys move us closer to a few other WannaBees. It's way too early for this. The sun hasn't even kissed the morning hello and we're standing in the dewy mist on the Great Lawn. And if I part my lips, I swear I can taste dawn.

I try again to give Gia and her posse of pink-and-gold Bees my undivided attention, but that's really hard. I spent the entire night replaying my walk with Dallas through the Daffodil Field over and over again. And then...over again.

Coach interrupts my stroll down memory lane when she taps on the microphone and commands our attention. "Girls, we have a little surprise for you before we get started." Then she nods at Gia and the squad. "The Honeys are coming around with your brand-new HoneyBee duffel bags. Inside you'll find your HoneyBee practice shorts and tees. We've also gifted you with a pair of pink-and-gold HoneyBee sweats for cold mornings like today."

Gia stands on her tippy-toes and takes the mic from Coach. "And MOST exciting...you'll each find a brand-new pair of pink-and-gold signature HoneyBee pom-poms."

The WannaBees don't waste any time grabbing their new duffels and unzipping them. Within seconds, the lawn is covered in pink-and-gold pom-poms. Giddy girls are trading tees, pulling on sweatpants, and taking selfies with their new haul. I reach into my bag and pull out Grammy Mae's fluffy pom-poms.

"Coach!" I yell to her as I approach the stage. "Uh, can I talk to you for a second?"

"Sure, Magic," she says, bending down to me. "What is it?"

I show her Grammy's poms. "These were my grandmother's pom-poms and I was wondering if I could use them instead of the new ones you just gave us."

71

Coach studies the poms. "Wow. I haven't seen a pair of these in ages. They're so—"

"Vintage," I spout, before she can say old.

"That's right, they are." She nods and then considers my unusual request. "Well, it's important that all the girls be uniform."

I glance at my hands and sigh.

"But seeing as how these are your grandmother's and she was one of the legendary HoneyBees on this very team, I don't see why we can't make an exception, especially just for practice. But if you make the team, you'll have to use the uniform poms."

I look up at her. "Really? Thanks, Coach. That means a lot to me and my family."

"Those are very special poms, Magic. And you're lucky to have them."

Her words replay in my mind about being lucky as I race back to my place in line.

"All right, girls!" Coach says, watching the Bees buzz through their new goodies. "Now that you have poms," she says, winking at me, "make sure you keep them with you, especially at workshops and practices. We are a pom-pom squad after all. Now let's get in formation and get back to making our championship squad the best it can be."

It isn't long before the excitement fades and my limbs turn to taffy. And one by one, we all drop like flies as they send us through a series of toe touches, jumps, rolls, kicks, flips, and extraterrestrial dance moves. By the fiftieth hip gyration, my ribs are on fire and my bad arm is throbbing again.

Cappie is right beside me, only she's intentionally dumbing down her dancing skills. She wants to make sure they put her in the same group as me, so she's pretending to be as challenged as I actually am.

"But you look silly, Capp," I say as her knees knock together and she shuffles her feet around and trips over herself, completely trash dancing.

"Dude, *The Magic Capricorn Show* must go on. I can't let you get stuck in a group alone. Without me."

I try not to laugh as she fumbles through her diagnostic, missing critical hip pops, double spins, and kick splits that I know she could do blindfolded.

"So much of this situation is wrong," Gia says as Cappie and I bump into each other during the high-kick routine. Gia nods at Yves, who slaps a yellow bee sticker over Cappie's HoneyBees tee. "And I thought you had real talent under that bad-girl exterior of yours," she says, spinning on her pink-and-gold platform booties. "I heard you were a divine dancer with ridiculous stunt potential. I guess everyone was wrong."

73

Cappie spits in the grass and shrugs.

"Seriously?!" Yves shrieks, covering her eyes.

"I guess those were all lies about you outperforming those D-list Disneys," Gia says, tapping her chin. "That's too bad, because that surfer bod of yours would look *amazy* in an HB uni."

It was true. Cappie had that toned surfer thing going and although she didn't make a point to show it off, she was proud of her athletic build and strength.

"But the truth is, you suck!" Gia taunts in Cappie's ear. Then she watches as I spin out of a pirouette and a chocolate chip breakfast muffin flies from the pocket of my hoodie. Gia shakes her head violently and presses a sticker on my back extra hard before dismissing me.

"That is all," she announces. And when I don't move, she spells it out for me. "I said, that is all!"

"Right," I say, shuffling away as Cappie makes rabbit ears behind Gia's head.

I tug at my sweater and see the yellow sticker. It's official. Cappie and I are both in the same group. We both laugh and slink through our secret Reptile handshake. Our plan is working, and for the first time, I start to feel good about my chances of surviving the next two weeks leading up to MidSummer cuts.

In the distance, I see three misfits sporting yellow

stickers making their way over to us. I'd seen two of them around the halls when we were in the sixth grade, but I didn't know their names.

A tiny girl with olive skin, silky dark hair, and abnormally big feet stumbles over her own shoe. That's when I spy a small earpiece lodged in her left ear. Cappie turns to me and points to the Honeys. "If they're the reigning HoneyBees—"

Another girl I'd never seen before is in a wheelchair. She shoots over to us and accidentally rolls over the toe of another girl I recognize with crazy cool cornrows.

"Ouch!" Cool Cornrows yells.

"Then we are clearly the StumbleBees." Cappie sighs.

"And they're the MayBees," I decide, looking at the really good dancers being gifted green stickers.

"This can't be good," Cappie finishes, watching the wheelchair get tangled in Cornrow's shoestring.

"Hi, I'm Brooklyn," Cool Cornrows says to me as she disentangles herself and walks up to us.

"Hi!" I pipe back.

She bends down to retie her shoe and nods to the girl with strawberry hair and freckles using the wheelchair. "And that's Winnie."

"Nice to meet you, Winnie," I say, offering my hand.

"You bet it is!" she says as I giggle-nod. "It's actually

Winfrey, but everyone calls me Winnie." Then she shrugs. "Your choice."

"Well, I'm Magic and"—I turn to Cappie, who forces a smile—"this is Capricorn."

But Cappie isn't too thrilled. I can hear her huffing in my ear as she forces a smile on her face, too.

"My homework name is Louise Chen," the tiny girl says, her hair cut into an enviable bob. "But you can call me LuLu, all my friends do." Then she twirls around our circle on her big tiptoes and says, "It's so cool to meet all of you. I'm so glad we're all in the same group!" Her hair swings around her shoulders.

Cappie leans over to me and whispers, "Is that a hearing aid in her ear?"

"Yeah," LuLu turns to her and answers. "It is."

"And obviously it works," Winnie snipes at Cappie.

"But don't worry, I can still hear the music," LuLu says, still sounding a little stiff. "But sometimes I might be a few beats behind. Not because of the hearing aid, but just because I'm not exactly the best dancer. But I'm a quick learner."

"I'm sure you'll catch up after we practice," Brooklyn says. "So while you're working on timing, I'll be working on my technique."

"And I'll be working on chair tricks," Winnie adds, popping her chair into a wheelie. But then she loses her balance and wobbles out of it. "Gotta build up these arms."

I stroke my chin and then I begin. "And I'll be working on, well...let's see, my turns and my kicks and my stunts and my dancing and my—"

Brooklyn interrupts my train of thought and soothes us all. "We've got two whole weeks to all get there for MidSummer and then another week for Finale. We can help each other!"

"A lot can happen in three weeks," LuLu says. "That's like...forever."

"Cappie, what are you going to be working on?"

But Cappie doesn't answer; instead, she sighs loudly and then nitpicks everyone under her breath. "A wheelchair, a hearing aid, and a—?" She stops when her eyes land on Brooklyn, who is break-dancing around Winnie and LuLu.

"I know, right!" I pep, beyond psyched about how different and special we all are. "Isn't it so cool!"

But Cappie ignores my excitement. Instead, her eyes dart across the lawn and land on the MayBees. And they're showing real promise. You can tell most of them had a dance background and could probably even push some of the reigning Bees out of the hive. Cappie watches as they finish their diagnostics. When the music starts again, she slips into a dance trance and starts jamming with them. Before I can stop Cappie, Yves nudges Gia and they glance over in her direction, just as Cappie flashes her poms and hits a perfect double pirouette.

"Cappie, you're totally showing off," I whisper-yell at her. "And they're watching you."

Gia and Yves tap Coach on the shoulder. But when she turns around, Cappie fake-falls to the ground. Then she hops back up and pretends to be dance-challenged again. But she doesn't seem as happy about it as she did earlier this morning.

I watch Gia and Yves go back and forth with each other before finally scribbling something on their clipboards. When they turn their backs to continue assigning green stickers to the MayBees, Cappie giggles. I force myself to join her, but it's different this time. I don't feel like we're in on the joke together. It's not as funny to me anymore, and I can't help feeling like a selfish friend. She deserves to be proudly wearing a green sticker with the rest of the MayBees, and I'm holding her back. Even though she doesn't seem to care today, how long will it be before she starts to resent me and my severe lack of dance ability?

Decided: I'm going to improve...fast! It's only a matter of time before the KillerBees discover Cappie's serious skills—if they haven't already. And I want to be ready to join her when she moves up.

My phone dings as D-Day wraps. A text pops onto the screen.

Dallas: Are you making Magic happen?

I fumble with the phone.

On the one hand, I promised Cappie that I'd stay far away from Boy Wonder. But on the other hand, maybe a small part of me (okay, a gigantic part) wants to know what it would be like to spend *more* time with him. I bite down on my lip and weigh my options. The bad angel knocks the good angel right off my shoulder and she tumbles to the ground. I can't help her now. I text him back.

Me: More like making TRAGIC happen!

Dallas: Want to enlist your personal trainer after dinner?

I glance at Cappie. This would be the second secret I've kept from her in my whole life. And both have to do with Dallas. I pinch my eyes shut and press SEND.

Me: I'M IN!

CHAPTER 9

"So how'd D-Day turn out?" Dallas asks when I meet him by a big oak tree at the end of the Daffodil Field.

I must've looked over my shoulder a million times walking over here. And I was almost in full disguise wearing oversized camouflage sweats. I even had a Valentine snapback pulled over my eyes. The hoodie was tied under my chin so the bottom half of my face was covered and all that was missing was a mustache and a fake nose. I couldn't risk Gia and her venomous Bees stinging me to death if they knew I was going to talk to her crush.

"I told you," I say as I stop next to him. "It was way tragic. I'm in the lowest group."

"I get that," he says, matter-of-fact, as I follow him over the hill and down the rocky path to the beach. "Those girls are local champions."

And evil villains.

"Where're we going anyway?" I whisper. I try to follow his lead and duck beneath a thorny bush. "I thought we weren't supposed to leave campus."

"I won't tell if you won't." He glances back at me and I try my best to disguise the grin that's covering my face.

"We're going down to the beach. It's my favorite spot." He grabs the bush before it can rebound and smack me in the face. "I guess you could say it's my happy place. I can really focus when I'm there." He looks past his shoulder at me. "I can trust you, right?" I nod as we step off the path and trudge through a tall patch of grass, straight into a big stretch of untouched sand and smooth pebbles.

"So, you're in the yellow group." He leans against a huge rock that reminds me of a spaceship.

"I didn't think anyone cared about how I was doing."

"I do." He smiles a different smile, one I hadn't seen before. "I watched you. You weren't as bad as you think you were." He starts stretching and nudges me to imitate his stretches. "Be careful not to hurt your arm again."

I try to get my head to touch my knee like his does.

But the back of my leg feels like it's being pulled tight like a brand-new rubber band. "I was pretty bad; you can admit it."

"Maybe you're not where you want to be, but everyone has to start somewhere." He motions for me to keep stretching. And what began as preventative injury stretches turns into fifteen minutes of power walking in the sand because "it revs up the workout." I'm walking as fast as I can while he's whizzing past me. Back and forth. And then back and forth again. I stop when my shoe gets stuck in the sand for the third time.

"Keep going," he yells after he finally stops at the lifeguard stand. "Don't stop. It'll slow your heart rate. Trust me, you can do this."

That's when I lose all feeling in my legs and collapse next to the seaweed. "What if the tide pulls me away because now I can't move?"

"Okay, I get it. You can stop walking now," he says when I crawl to the lifeguard stand to join him. "And since you're already down there," he says, watching me roll around in the sand. "Let's try fifty crunches. But you can make them the girly ones. Just raise your head to the sky and tighten your core."

I have no idea how to do a crunch. Not even a girly one. I mean, I've eaten my fair share of Nestlé Crunches, sure, but I've never actually *done* one. So I watch him demonstrate a proper girl-crunch, but it's no use because now I can't stop thinking about chocolate.

"Your turn," he says, and watches me struggle to lift my head out of the sand.

If I'm being honest, this particular maneuver seems dumb. I feel like a woodpecker drilling my beak into an imaginary tree.

"Okay, we'll get back to those," he says after my fifth try, giving up on my ridiculous pecking.

"Thanks for understanding that I'm dying," I say, and hobble back to the spaceship rock.

"No, you're not. It just feels like it. And that's because you're new to this."

I think I'm going to be sick. "Uh-oh." That's when I feel my eyes roll around inside my head. I look away from him, crouch into the fetal position, and clutch my belly. And before I can catch myself, I'm vomiting in the sand.

"Sweet!" he yells, kneeling down next to me and grabbing a handful of my hair in his hands. "Sometimes the body responds this way, especially when you're not used to it. Try not to freak out."

I glance up at Dallas, who's now protecting my sweaty

curls from chunks of extra cheesy pepperoni pizza. I'm beyond humiliated mainly because this is happening in front of him and then because, well, it's happening at all.

"Sorry," I say, and wipe my mouth. "That's so embarrassing."

"You know, you're not the first person to struggle through a workout."

I fold my arms over my chest. "Like you know anything about it."

He leans back on his elbows and nods. "I remember when my dad was first teaching me how to catch a football. The ball was in the air and I ran toward it instead of waiting for it to come to me. And I swear, I only took my eyes off that thing for one second."

I cover my mouth. "And then you missed the catch?"

"Even worse." He giggles. "When I finally looked up at the ball, it smacked me right in the face."

This time I gasp. "No way!"

"Yep. My face turned purple and the ball smashed my eyeglasses into pieces."

"Ouch!" I shake my head. "Wait. *You* used to wear glasses?"

"Not after that." He chuckles at the memory. "My mom took me straight to the doctor to get contacts."

"I can't picture you with glasses."

"What about braces?" he says, laughing even harder. "But let's keep that between us." Before long, we're both laughing out loud, holding our bellies, and howling at the moon. And according to my count, I'm up to three Dallas Chase secrets.

CHAPTER 10

I creep back into my dorm, repeating the steps I took the night before. But this time, I know I've already missed curfew by thirty minutes. Hopefully Coach has gotten distracted and hasn't checked my room yet. Maybe one of the other girls was homesick. Or food sick. Or flu sick. I don't need one more hurdle to jump over tonight. Juggling Dallas, Gia, and now Cappie is exhausting.

After taking the back stairs, two at a time, I slip into my room. The lights are off, so I stand in the doorway. Perfectly still. And I listen for her snores.

"Magic. Olive. Poindexter. Again?"

I flip on the lights. "Hi, Mom." I try to get her to laugh. Or giggle. I'd even settle for a snortle.

"You missed curfew and I don't know where you were, but I definitely know who you were with," she says, scrambling to her feet. "You're lucky Coach believed me when I told her you were stuck in the bathroom with pepperoni pizza backfiring on you."

Well, that part was certainly true.

"You were gone for a whole hour and a half!" She tosses my pj's at me. I hold them up and Minnie Mouse's faded face stares back at me before I change into them.

"Okay." I glance at the floor. "Don't be mad, Capp, but maybe...we worked out."

Cappie swipes her finger at my mouth and sniffs it. "Let's see, a mix of peanut butter cup with a hint of Twizzler with lingering notes of—wait—is that *upchuck*?"

"Post workout vom."

"Ew." She snorts. "So you went behind my back and broke our pinkie swear."

"It's just that Dallas texted me and I really wanted to go. But I don't want you to be mad at me." Instead of looking at Cappie, I turn and bunch my salty, frizzy hair into a clip and push my feet into my Bugs Bunny slippers.

Cappie crosses her arms. "I don't understand why you chose him to help you over me anyway."

Memories of my surfboard slamming into my head as I floated around the Pacific Ocean alone rush back to me. I don't want that happening again, so I take a deep breath and finally blurt it out. "It's just that you aren't always the most patient bestie, Cappie, especially when it takes me a while to learn stuff. You know I love you, but sometimes that makes me not want to work with you."

I watch her eyes soften and the corners of her usually snarky smile turn upside down. For the first time since never I see what I think are her feelings. And they're hurt. But now I'm way confused because Cappie doesn't get hurt, she gets even. This is brand-spanking-new territory for our friendship, and I'm not sure what to say or do.

"Okay then," she says. "Show me the stuff we learned today. I'll help you and you'll see that I can be as patient as you need me to be. I'll even record it so you can see for yourself where you need to improve," she says, taking out her phone and pressing RECORD.

"Like now?" I say, thinking about my wobbly legs. "Like right now?"

She turns on some hip-hop music, keeping the volume low so we don't get in trouble. Then she motions for me to stand in front of her in the tight space between our bunks. "Uh-huh. Show me what you got."

After a few deep breaths, I give in and drag my feet

over to my duffel. I pull out my poms as she counts, "Five-six…five-six-seven-eight."

I can barely remember the first two eight-counts and when I do remember a sequence, I screw it up by bumping into her several times during the complex footwork. I mean, c'mon, it involved two twisted grapevine thingies called pas de bourrée and a backward piqué turn that's basically a spin on your tippy-toes with one foot resting at your ankle. And then that leads into a hip lunge. I try to chassé, which is just a fancy gliding step, across the room into the leap-jump, but I can't catch any air beneath me. And then after all that, I lose my balance and crash into my nightstand. That's when Grammy Mae's poms tumble right into my lap.

"Magic, keep going."

"Nah, I think I'm going to stay down here for a while." And I don't move. Mainly because my feet feel like they're glued to the floor and the rest of my body is relieved.

"You were doing it all wrong," Cappie says.

"Yeah, I figured that much."

"This isn't funny, Magic. Time is ticking. Only two weeks till MidSummer, where they'll make first cuts." She puts the phone on the dresser and fluster-sighs. "And you're not even trying."

"I am trying," I sulk. "See, this is what I mean about you not being patient. It's only the first day! Dallas didn't—" But I don't dare say another word; instead, I get up and head for the sink to brush my teeth. Then I try to explain one more time. "I know you won't believe me, Capp, but we have a lot of things in common."

"You and Boy Wonder?" she scoffs before reaching for her phone. "You should hear yourself. He's more like me than you know," she mocks, recording me again.

"Seriously, Capp. I've never been around a boy like him before. He talks to me like I'm a real person." Toothpaste flies out of my mouth and lands on her brow. "And he's interested in stuff about me, and not because of who my dad is or because he played basketball," I continue. "He didn't even ask for his autograph."

"Okay," she says, wiping her eyebrow with the back of her hand. "But—"

"And when he talks to me, he looks right into my eyes." I spit into the sink and spin back around to her as water drips from my chin. "Like he's really looking at *me*." I hold Barkley up to show her. "Like this," I say, looking lovingly into my teddy bear's eyes. Cappie steadies the phone in her hand and tries not to laugh. But in my opinion, she doesn't try hard enough. "See, I told you. I knew you wouldn't understand."

She tosses her phone onto her bed and slinks into a yoga pose. "Enough about loverboy. You let me know when you're ready to practice and give it your all. In the meantime, I'll be over here in Lotus Pose."

Grammy Mae's poms are watching me from the floor. And I can hear Mom's voice in my head explaining to me just how special they are. I crawl into the bed with them and settle in next to Barkley. "I'm pooped. Let's call it a night and try this again another time. Pretty please."

Cappie scratches her head as she walks across the room and flips off the light switch. "You've got a lot of work to do, Magic. How are we ever going to get you ready?"

That's when I spy a little twinkle in the handles of the poms. And when I pull back the pink-and-gold streamers, that same golden glow swirls around Grammy Mae's initials: HMJ.

Maybe I do have a lot of work ahead of me, but it's the same work that Grammy Mae had before her. If she could do it with these pom-poms by her side, maybe I can, too.

CHAPTER 11

LET'S GO, HONEYBEES, LET'S GO!

The HoneyBees double clap their pom-poms, swarming in and out of two overlapping pink-and-gold circles as they belt out one of their spirit chants.

LET'S GO, HONEYBEES, LET'S GO!

Gia and Yves take turns perfecting back handsprings into somersaults across the lawn as two almost-identical Honeys, Sammie and Tabitha, basket toss a mini stunter through the air. Their blond, shoulder-length hair doesn't make them stand out from the rest of the team, but their strong arms definitely catch my attention.

Capricorn and I run toward the Great Lawn. I watch as the stunter tumbles toward the sky, then descends straight into a perfect toe touch and lands in Sammie's and Tabitha's arms. *Holy stunt girls!*

It's a struggle for me to even move my legs this morning. And my neck is even stiffer than my arms. It's like my entire body has been slow roasting in the oven. And I feel throbby. And tight. And wobbly.

Before I can catch my breath, another group of Honeys lifts a flyer straight into a gravity-defying pose. And they're holding her feet in the palms of their hands.

"What in the world!" I yell as the topper arches her back and holds one leg at a ninety-degree angle behind her head while she balances all her weight on her other leg. And all I can think is *Whoa!*

"Did you see that?" I spazz to Cappie and wave Grammy's poms in the air.

She grabs my arm and pulls me close. "That's called a Scorpion. And keep up, we're already nine minutes late."

But I don't hurry; in fact, I freeze when that same girl straightens her leg and holds it all the way behind her back, almost pressing her heel to her ear. And she doesn't fall.

94

"Cappie! Did you see that one?"

"That's the Straight Leg Scorpion," she says, grabbing me and pulling me toward the Great Lawn. "And now we're ten minutes late!"

Now eleven whole minutes late, Cappie and I run toward the StumbleBees as they wave us over. And when we finally catch up to them, Winnie rolls her chair to the right so Cappie and I can squeeze in.

"Did we miss anything?" I ask Brooklyn, pulling Grammy Mae's poms from my bag.

"Nope, just the Honeys showing off how amazing they are." I think Brooklyn's pretty great herself. She has those gymnast arms that I'm sure muscle-flex when she raises her hand in class. "Coach didn't even take roll yet." She spins around and does a slick break dance move before pointing at the pom-poms in my hand. "Love those. Are they vintage?"

"They were my Grammy Mae's," I answer, pushing my shoulders back. "She was a cheerleader at Valentine back in the day. In fact, she was the first Black cheerleader on the team. She made big moves and she always said she saw so much of herself in me. And, well, I want to be just like her."

"Way cool."

"But this superhard stunt and pom routine is the

95

opposite of cool," I admit, feeling like I'll never be able to master any of it. It involves high kicks and something called Herkies, where you kick your leg up in the front and back at the same time but you bend the back one. Then to add on to that, Brooklyn makes sure to tell me to double down on the beat.

"What's that even mean?" I ask her as I try to repeat the spastic moves to the five-six-seven-and-eight counts.

"It's when you put two dance moves on one beat. It's sick, but only when you do it right." I can tell by her expression that she didn't think I was doing it right. "Otherwise, it just looks dumb. Not that you look dumb, of course!"

Two moves on one beat? I can barely put one foot in front of the other this morning. It feels like my muscles are on strike.

While Brooklyn is picking up some of the moves, Winnie is trying to swing her chair around and land on the seven-eight count, but she can't seem to get it around in time. And LuLu isn't doing much better. Whenever she ends up two beats behind the captain, she swats her hand into the air like she's fighting a mosquito.

But guess who's the most dance-challenged? Yep, me!

No matter how hard I try, I can't get my arms and legs to stop flailing in the wind. I look like one of those inflatable tubes flapping around outside of the car dealerships. And Cappie won't stop laughing, even though she looks pretty funny, too, pretending to be stuck in the grass like a slug.

"Ooh, look, G, our resident Tragic is here," Yves announces to Gia as they approach us. "Tragic Magic and Kettle Corn decided to grace us with their presence."

"Too bad they didn't bring Talent and Rhythm with them." Gia turns to me and fake-smiles. Then she squints her eyes at the poms in my hands. "Where did you get those dusty old things? Those are *not* signature HoneyBee poms."

"They were my grandmother's," I say, riding onto my tiptoes and grinning.

Gia giggle-snorts into the air. "Was she like one hundred?"

"They're vintage," Brooklyn boasts.

"They're ancient." Yves snorts.

"Coach said I can use them."

Everyone turns to look at my poms. The KillerBees and some of the MayBees are snickering and pointing at them. I can hear their voices sweep across the lawn.

"Where did she get those things?"

"They're so big and ... ugly."

"They actually fit you perfectly," Gia says. "Out of style and way uncool—just like you."

"My grandmother made history at Valentine Middle," I scoff at the Killers. "She made a way for girls who look like me to be on that court. And I want to make her proud."

But instead of Gia and Yves applauding my legacy, they just point and laugh at the poms.

"You probably should've left them in the room," Cappie says, halfway scolding me.

That's when Yves snaps her fingers at me and hisses, "No one would think you're a loser if you just ran home to Mommy and Daddy. Your sister is a legend, but you— you have no business being here."

"I'm not going anywhere," I mutter under my breath, thinking these girls should be captains of a team called the VenomBees and not the HoneyBees because these girls are the antonym of sweet.

After practice, Winnie, Lu, and Brooklyn decide to go with Cappie and me to the café for lunch.

"You know, Magic," Winnie says, rolling through a path in the Daffodil Field. "I think your gramma's poms are seriously cute. They're all big and bouncy."

"And crinkly," Brooklyn adds.

"Yeah. What do Gia and Yves know anyway?" LuLu

98

skips through the field, waving her finger in the air. "Retro is so in right now. And all my fashion girl Instagram feeds would argue that it never really went out of style in the first place."

"Don't take it personally, Magic. She's just mad because she doesn't come from a legacy like yours," Brooklyn explains. "Cheerleading is all she has to feel good about herself." Her voice lowers. "I heard that her mom doesn't even come to any of her games."

"And I bet your whole family will show up for every one of yours," Winnie says.

"She just wants a family like yours," says Brooklyn. "You were gifted your grandmother's pom-poms, for crying out loud. Talk about support! She's just jealous."

"I didn't know that about her," I say, suddenly staring at my feet. "I mean, that sucks—I even kind of feel bad for her! But I still wish I didn't have this target on my back."

Brooklyn huffs, "Me too. But I'm pretty sure we all share that same target right about now. That's why they put us in a group together. We stand out. None of us are like the other girls here."

"Tell me about it," Winnie agrees.

"Yeah," LuLu cosigns.

"Well," Brooklyn says, rocking onto her tiptoes. "I'm

happy to stand out. I wouldn't want to be like those captains. I like being *me*, the girl obsessed with selling Girl Scout cookies and break dancing. Some of the girls think selling cookies is a chore, but I have a master plan."

"You're a Girl Scout?" LuLu asks.

"Oh my gosh," I say as I rub my hands together. "Can you get us boxes of cookies? Thin Mints are my fave! But I love the Do-si-dos, too."

"I sure am." Brooklyn stands up tall and proud. "And I was a Brownie before that. And this year, I even came in second for selling the most cookies in my district. Next year, I'm going to beat everyone and expand my cookie empire."

I high-five her. "So, you're a break-dancing businesswoman."

"I like that." She laughs as she nods. "I plan on going to college on a dance scholarship, and then to business school. I want to do it all. And I don't see why I can't."

"And you probably want to be a princess when you grow up, too," Cappie says, ragging on her.

"Nope." Brooklyn flexes her arm muscle. "I want to be a king."

"I can relate," Winnie says. "I love doing more than one thing, too. I have a passion for acting *and* playing the piano."

I pretend to stroke the imaginary piano keys across the tops of the daffodils. "You know how to play an instrument?"

"Yep. But I want to learn guitar next. Or maybe the drums. But I have to balance it with theater. At my old school, I was in the drama club. I love acting in school plays. I was the Wicked Witch of the West in our last production."

We all check Winnie out like we're seeing her for the first time.

"I can see that," Cappie says, nodding. But her voice is dripping with sarcasm. "You'd make a good witch."

Winnie ignores Cappie's snark and brushes her shoulders off with pride. "You better believe I did. And now I'm working on finishing my first play. Before I came to camp, I started writing it. I'm calling it *Wheels in the City*."

"Sounds like you're a real writer," LuLu says. "I write, too. Mostly about fashion, but sometimes I try poetry and short stories. I've almost filled up ten journals."

"Maybe we can write something together one day," Winnie says.

LuLu lights up and fist-bumps Winnie. "Now that would be cool!"

"And I could put a business strategy together and sell it to everyone," Brooklyn pipes up. "Just like my cookies."

"And maybe I could design the website. I'm learning coding," I say, offering my services. "I'm actually going to coding camp after we finish at Planet Pom-Poms."

Winnie twirls her curls like she's in deep thought. "We'll need a website for sure."

"And tons of social media," Brooklyn adds, pointing at me.

"I'm your girl," I boast. "And Cappie can help, too."

But Cappie doesn't agree to any of it. In fact, she just keeps walking so fast that she's now several steps ahead of us—passing the football field.

"See, we don't need to be like the captains," Winnie declares. "We've got our own thing going on. And together, I'm sure we can do anything, even make the HoneyBees team."

"But you guys are in the yellow group!" Cappie yells over her shoulder. "You do know they think you're the ones with the least amount of talent, right?"

"What do they know? We're going to work really hard and show them what we can do," Brooklyn corrects Cappie. "We all love dancing and cheering, too."

"Besides, look at all the cool stuff we've already accomplished," Winnie says. "By the time camp is over, we could be unstoppable!"

That's when Cappie rolls her eyes and groans up at the sky. "But you guys are the StumbleBees."

"You mean *we* are the StumbleBees. You're one of us, too," LuLu says.

We all nod and tighten our circle to stretch our arms into the middle, and it reminds me of my family. I giggle as we pile our hands on top of each other.

Everyone except Cappie.

That's when I clear my throat and nod for her to join us. When she doesn't budge, I just blurt out, "Cappie!" until she finally gives in and plops her arm on top of the heap.

"Who are we?" Brooklyn peps. "I said, WHO ARE WE?!"

We all bounce up and down, each of us on our own unique beat. And then we scream, "The StumbleBees!"

CHAPTER 12

Later at lunch, Cappie and I are stuck at the buffet because I'm holding up the line, trying to grab everything. I push a tray of deliciousness along the assembly line. And it couldn't have come any sooner. I'm pretty sure my stomach was starting to eat itself. After that last sideline chant at practice, Gia's head was beginning to look like a meatball and her arms and legs like stringy spaghetti. Cappie sighs over my shoulder because I'm taking longer than everyone else to fix my plate.

Mashed potatoes. Check.

Bacon double cheeseburger. Check.

Sweet potato fries. Check.

Chicken nuggets. Check.

More chicken nuggets. Double check.

Cappie douses her salad with the dark purple vinai-grette on the counter and I dunk my nuggets into my saucer of barbecue sauce. Then we both look around the café for a place to sit. "Everyone's already cliqued up again," she says, pointing to two tables of girls. "Over there, some of the HoneyBees and then next to them, a few of the MayBees."

But then I point to LuLu and Brooklyn sitting down at a table next to Winnie.

"Great." Cappie sighs. "The StumbleBees again."

I happily push Cappie toward their table and she reluctantly trudges along.

I giggle when I see Winnie on the end, eating Fla-min' Hot Cheetos with one hand and salad with the other. Between bites, she's deep in conversation with LuLu. They're bickering about the models in LuLu's lat-est Instagram story. I'm all ears when I realize their dis-cussion involves french fries.

"Eat this," Winnie says, and drops a handful of french fries onto LuLu's plate. "Those models are all photo-shopped to death. None of the stuff on your fashion IG feed is real!"

LuLu smells the fries instead. I fight the urge to eat

them myself. I'd never let hot french fries go to waste (or cold ones either).

Brooklyn ignores them. Instead, she's at the far end of the table listening to her jumbo headphones, practicing in her seat the choreography we learned today. She's not at all concerned if anyone sees her dancing or rapping to her pepperoni.

Winnie spins around in her chair. "Hey, we thought you'd never leave that buffet table." I laugh as I scoot into the seat beside her and make room for Cappie.

Brooklyn stops dancing and shoves her headphones onto her neck. She looks like she has something serious to say. We all stop to listen. "Hey, Cappie, weren't you a Disney star when you were little?"

"She was a Nick baby, not Disney," Winnie says, clearing it up for the table. "She was on that show *Rainbow*, with those dancing kids and that flying cat, Oscar."

"Ohhh," Brooklyn and Lu sing in unison.

"Then what're you doing in our group?" Winnie opens another bag of Flamin' Hot Cheetos and turns it upside down. Most of the orange chips scatter around her plate but two of them land in her kale. She tosses them into her salad without a second thought. "I watched you on that show when you were little. You guys always danced at the end of each episode."

"Now I remember. But wasn't it a flying dog?" Brooklyn rubs her chin and squints her eyes. She looks like she's picturing a dog sitting right next to her.

Winnie chomps on a chip. "No, it was a cat, for sure. I remember because it always purred when the credits rolled."

Cappie shrugs. She usually doesn't like talking about her past. She always says, "It's not reflective of where I am today, ya know?" But she was on TV, for crying out loud. That's supreme! But I try and support her choice to not talk about it.

Fortune always tells her to be nice to her fans, and not to get her panties in a bunch. I don't get that either, but no matter what, I do support Fortune not wanting Cappie's panties in her butt.

LuLu stares at my plate. She's totally hypnotized. "I'd kill to be able to eat like that. My mom never lets me eat junk food."

I take three nuggets from my plate and place them on hers. "Good thing she's not here."

"She says I'll need a husband more than I'll ever need carbs," LuLu says, staring at the nuggets.

"You're twelve, Lu," Winnie says. "Why are you even thinking about a husband?"

"Actually, I'm eleven. And I already know I like these

better than lip gloss." LuLu giggles and scarfs the nuggets down. "OMG. *Seriously?* Why didn't somebody tell me they were this yum?" Her eyes glaze over. "These are even better than buying new bronzer at Sephora."

"I know, right!" I say, shoveling two more into my own face. "Wait. What's bronzer?"

LuLu scrolls through her YouTube channel to a makeup tutorial and points to the shimmery stuff that looks like glittery blush.

"Ohhh," I say. "My big sister, Fortune, loves that stuff."

"It's gorge, especially on high cheekbones like yours."

I grab my spoon and check out my reflection on the back of it. I suck in my cheeks and poke my finger into them. "I never knew I had good cheekbones."

"Yeah, they're everything. Look how defined they are, and with some bronzer, they'd pop even more."

I turn to Cappie. "Hey, did you know I have pop-able cheekbones?"

But she rolls her eyes. "Who are you turning into?" she spews at me. "The old Magic would never care about bone structure."

Just as I'm about to crack a lame science joke about the skeletal system, the HoneyBees march into the café. And just like that, everyone stops chewing. We all watch as they glide to their table, in perfect unison, wearing their matching workout gear with slicked back ponytails and pink-and-gold bows in their hair.

"We can be HoneyBees, too. We just have to make it past MidSummer, guys," Brooklyn says.

LuLu nods. "None of us better get cut."

"Practice is the name of the game," Brooklyn adds. "If we keep working at it every day, I think we really have a shot. Even me!"

"But you're a killer dancer," I say to her. "I still don't really understand why you're in our group. I mean, I saw you with my own eyes!"

"Yep, I can rock with the best *street* dancers," she agrees, before beatboxing and drumming her hands on the table. Then she twists her body into a cool pose and snakes out of it. But when she awkwardly attempts a ballerina stance with her arms, she sighs. "But I've got zero technique."

We all nod in agreement, everyone understanding what it's like to lack technique.

"I've been dreaming of being a HoneyBee for a long time, too, Lu," Winnie says. "They're the reigning district champions. And they'll probably beat everyone at Regionals next year."

"They're the best. And we would add *so* much flavor

to that squad," Brooklyn says, marking an eight-count from the choreography. When she raises her arm into a high V, her muscles flex.

"Those are real muscles," I say before I have a second to think about it. "I mean . . . you're so fit and strong."

"That's mainly because of my workout plan."

"Like . . . you do jumping jacks and girly push-ups and stuff like that?"

Cappie snarls loud enough for the entire table to hear. But Brooklyn giggles in a cool-girl way. "Yeah, I definitely do stuff like that. And other stuff, too."

I hard-swallow the nuggets I just popped into my mouth. "And your arms probably give you serious Olympic strength."

"Yours could, too, ya know."

Brooklyn grabs my arm and makes a lazy muscle. "See, you could get there. With some stuff like push-ups and weight training, you could become strong enough to hold up a few of those HoneyBees in a cheer stunt."

I giggle-snort. "No way."

"Girl, if you can learn to code, you can do anything you put your mind to. And if you want, I could show you."

Cappie bites off the asparagus on her fork and then stabs the fork into her plate. When I look at her, she rolls her eyes and whispers into my ear, "I thought training you was my job. Now you're giving it to someone else. *Again.*"

I turn back to Brooklyn. "You don't have to do that."

"No biggie. Somebody showed me how to train," she says. "I'm down to pay it forward."

"Uh, well—"

And before I can answer, Cappie gets up from the table and walks away. But not before turning back to me to whisper in my ear, "Who *are* you?"

I look up at her and answer, "I'm a StumbleBee."

CHAPTER 13

The sign on the oversized double doors says:

GYM

That's when I hear the steel doors open. Without thinking, I shuffle backward into the bushes and my duffel gets tangled in all the greenery. From behind the vines, I spy two HoneyBees prancing in my direction. I peer through the shrubbery and watch as they toss their cheer bags over their shoulders and skip right past me toward the Great Lawn. *How many more of them are in there? What if it's the whole team?*

"Magic!" Brooklyn says, jogging up to me. "Perfect timing."

I grab a handful of branches and shove them out of the way. "I was, uh, just... Have you checked out these leaves?" I pull two leaves from the bush and then I don't know what to do with them so I just drop them. "And fun fact: The HoneyBees are all here."

Brooklyn opens the heavy door and shrugs at me. "It's the gym, so yeah, that makes sense. They have work to do, too."

Coach explained at the start of camp that our afternoon gym workouts are optional. Even though she and the stunt trainers said they'd be in the gym if we decided to exercise, it wasn't a requirement. So, needless to say, I'm shocked to see so many faces in workout gear coming and going as I tiptoe into the building.

"All these people actually *want* to be here?" I yell to Brooklyn as I follow her down the hall and around the corner. We head into a big room with a colorful climbing wall that's almost touching the ceiling and tons of metal workout machines that look like Transformers.

Coach waves at us from the water fountain, and then she motions for us to join her.

"Good to see you, girls," she says, typing into her iPad. "And what are you going to be working on today?"

"We'll just be stretching and weight training," Brooklyn explains. "It's my normal routine when I work out with my dad."

"It's not my normal routine," I quickly add. "But I want to work on getting stronger."

Coach rubs my shoulders and smiles. "You know, you'd be a great base for the team, Magic. They stand at the bottom of the stunts and make sure the girl on top doesn't fall. They're the whole foundation of our stunts."

My eyes light up at the thought of having such an important job. "You really think so?"

She nods and pats my shoulder. Then she says, "There are three trainers in that section. They'll help you girls get set up."

"Come on," Brooklyn says when she catches me staring at all the machines. "Let's head over to the mats and stretch before hitting it."

I'm wondering what, exactly, we're going to be hitting when two more shiny HoneyBees in matching pink leggings and strappy sports tops waltz past. But before I can find a suitable hiding spot, they don't waste any time pointing and giggling at me.

I follow their pointy fingers and look down at my wrinkled Valentine tee and my gold gym shorts that Principal Pootie insists that we wear for class or else he sends a note home to our parents. I eye my thick black socks and heavy white sneakers. And then I shrug, mainly because I don't understand what's so funny. This is how I always dress for gym class.

"Magic, what's wrong?" Brooklyn asks, doubling back to grab me.

"It's just that sometimes it's easy to shrug off the teasing and laughing at me. But then other times..." I sigh. "Have you ever had that feeling like you just want to disappear...you know, become completely invisible?"

"Oh yeah. I know that feeling." She nods, watching the HoneyBees dance around the corner and down the hall. "But try not to think about them. They're just background noise." She drops her duffel on the floor, grabs my hand, and pulls me down to the mats with her.

"They're what?"

"Background noise. It's like they really don't matter," she says, nodding for emphasis. "That's just something my dad says whenever I start to get overwhelmed with too many thoughts in my head." Then she takes off her shoes, spreads her legs apart, and twists her body around to one side. "Just follow what I do. But try to listen to your body—you don't want to push too hard in your first session."

"What is my body supposed to say to me?"

"Wait a minute," Brooklyn says, gawking at me. "Have you really never worked out before?"

I mute the loud memory of Dallas Chase, the sand, and the starry beach. "If you don't count gym class, then one whole time," I say proudly. "But I don't think I did it right. There was vomit involved."

"Yuck," she shrieks, fake-shivering.

"You're telling me."

"Working out can actually be fun. For me, it's a chance to get out of my head and not think about the bad stuff. And I always feel better when I'm done."

"Will I feel better, too?"

"Well, I can promise there won't be any vomiting involved," she says, easing me into a simple leg stretch.

The girls next to me grunt through their workout. And none of it sounds fun.

"Just trust me. Try to think of your muscles like rubber bands. And we definitely don't want them to snap." She leans over and presses her head into her kneecap.

I follow her lead and twist my body around until I look like a contortionist on the outside, but on the inside, I'm dying to ask her more about that noise in her head. Sometimes I have lots of thoughts, too, but they're usually about chocolate or science questions or some combination of both. Is that normal?

Three more Honeys are working out on machines that look like moving escalators.

"And *that's* going to help me get stronger? A moving escalator?" I say.

"The StairMaster is just one way to get stronger. There are others. You just gotta put in the work. And we're going to do exactly that. Then we'll make our own history."

"I like the way that sounds." It's nice to have someone beside me who is encouraging, even though I'm still super nervous about all of this.

"My dad always says there's room for her-story." She victory-smiles and points at me, and then back to herself.

"If we work really hard to make the team and then Winnie and LuLu do, too, every girl at Valentine Middle will be able to see themselves out there on that court."

"I bet that definitely hasn't happened before."

"And I think it's time we do something about it. You down for that?" she asks, not really asking, and heads to a machine with a seat and a bar across the middle. The trainer steps up and helps her adjust the weights. Then he steps back and motions for me to take his spot.

"I can't wait for you to try this one," Brooklyn says, sliding into the seat and rubbing it lovingly. "This one's my baby."

I exhale and walk over to her. "What does it do?"

She pulls the metal bar down to her chest. "It's good for your biceps and tris."

When she notices that my brows are arched into my hairline she says, "Your triceps." She pokes the back of my arms. "These right here. And when yours get strong, you'll be able to lift the flyers when we stunt. My dad started me on this machine earlier this year when I turned twelve."

"Is your dad like your personal coach or something?" I ask, watching her lift the metal bar up and down until she finally yells out, "Fifteen!" Then she wriggles out of the seat and wipes it off before pointing for me to sit down. "He's a football coach for the boys' league at the neighborhood rec center." She points at the seat. Again.

"You really want me to do that?"

"Yep," she says, taking all the weight off it. "Lift it up and down ten times. That'll make one set with ten reps. We'll build from there."

But I don't move.

"Trust me." She giggles. "You can do it. You're stronger than you think." She lifts the handlebar with one hand. "See. There's nothing on it anymore, so it should just feel like you're lifting your backpack."

I close my eyes and muster all my might. And then I pull the bar toward my chest.

"You're totally lifting weights, Magic! You're an official weight lifter as of right"—she checks her watch—"now!" I watch her add on three pounds. "Keep going. Now it should feel more like a fat cat."

I watch the three-pound weight bar go up and down until she counts to ten. "Is your mom into fitness?" I ask. And almost immediately, I watch her shoulders drop. Within seconds, her energy drops, too.

"Brooklyn? What's the matter? Did I say something wrong?"

She shakes her head. Then she just sighs. "It's just that...well...my mom's not here anymore."

"Where is she?" By the time I realize I've put my foot deep into my mouth, it's too late to take it out.

"She died. This year."

"Oh!" I stop lifting the stupid bar. "I'm so sorry. Me and my big mouth should probably mind our own business."

Brooklyn shifts her weight around. "It's okay. I mean, it's not but—"

"We don't have to talk about it if you don't want to," I say, the words rushing out of my mouth.

Brooklyn looks at me, then she looks away. "I haven't really talked about this stuff with anyone before."

"I'm a really good listener," I say. "My teddy bear Barkley tells me that all the time."

"You're something else, Magic," Brooklyn says, laughing.

"And I'm here for you—if you need a new friend. I only really have Cappie, so I definitely have room."

I watch Brooklyn stare at her sneakers. And since she doesn't say anything, I don't either. Then she takes a deep breath and whispers, "She died in January."

"Wow. I'm so sorry. That's a big deal."

"No one really knows. I'm still learning how to deal with it myself."

"I bet that's really hard. You're even stronger than I thought."

"It *is* really hard. She was my best friend."

"That's how I felt about my Grammy Mae. And then I lost her, too." I pat Brooklyn on the back. "Do you want to talk about your mom? Talking to my big sister, Fortune, always makes me feel better."

Brooklyn sighs. "I haven't really talked about her since the funeral." She shrugs and looks into the distance like she's far away. And after a few quiet minutes, she tunes back in. "But maybe talking about her wouldn't be a bad thing."

"What was your favorite thing about her?" I ask.

"My favorite? There were too many to count!"

"I bet," I say, smiling. "Tell me *all* of them."

"Well, one thing I used to love a lot was the way her voice sounded. She had this raspy voice that was really sweet but really firm at the same time. And she could sing, too. Whenever I was having a bad day or if I was sick, she would tuck me into bed with her and sing old songs. And her voice always made them sound so cool."

"She sounds special."

"She was." And then she doesn't say anything else. And I don't want to push, so I just say, "I'm here if you ever want to tell me more about her. I'd love to listen."

That's when she wipes her eye. But she doesn't cry. And I'm glad because I didn't want to make her sad.

I look around the gym and then I tell her, "I know I was nervous at first, but thanks for sharing this with me." I grab her hand. "And for sharing all of that other stuff, too."

She squeezes my hand back. "Thanks for listening."

"Anytime," I say to my new friend. "Any. Time."

So far being twelve is stacking up to be a doozy. I look around the gym and somehow, for the first time, all the Transformer machines and the climbing wall and the weights don't seem so scary anymore.

CHAPTER 14

A few days later, the Bees are all sprawled across the Great Lawn for another gut-wrenching practice. As usual, we're starting with stretches, and honestly, I down-right hate this part. And so does every part of my body. I'm sure you can imagine how torturous it is when I have to spread my legs far apart and bury my head in the grass in front of me.

"Good job, girls!" Coach announces to everyone from the stage on the Great Lawn. "Now take a quick break if you need one, grab your water, and finish your stretching so we can get into the signature HoneyBee routine."

"I hate this stretch!" I complain to the Stumbles.

Coach told us that it's the best way to prevent injuries, but right now, I'm feeling like an injury wouldn't be so bad if it means I won't have to finish stretching.

"Close your eyes and breathe in as you push your belly toward the ground," Brooklyn says. "Then exhale slowly. Just like we did at the gym the other day."

"I feel like one of those twisted balloon animals," I yell back at her. "And if you push my belly any lower, I think I might actually pop."

"We all look like twisted balloons," Winnie says, giggling. "I think I should be an elephant. They have good memories, just like me."

"And I'll be a giraffe," LuLu pipes in. "Because they have nice long necks. And long necks are all the rage."

We giggle together and check out the other girls on the Great Lawn, deciding what twisted balloon animals they should be, too.

"Eightttttttt...niiiiiine...," Gia counts, taking her sweet time getting to ten while my legs are threatening to snap.

I watch as Cappie stretches like a pro. She keeps looking at me and then looking away. I pretend like I don't know what's wrong, but deep down I do. She's still miffed because I worked out with Brooklyn instead of her. I kind of get why she's in her feelings, but then when

I really think about it, Cappie doesn't even *like* working out at the gym; yoga is her jam.

Meanwhile, my legs are trembling, and my back is even starting to burn.

"And ten!" Gia finally peps.

The sea of WannaBees exhales, and on cue, we all massage our legs back to life. I'm finally starting to feel my blood rush back to my head when Coach yells, "Grab your pom-poms and hop to your feet, girls! The captains are going to take you through the signature HoneyBee routine. This is what you'll be performing at MidSummer, so pay attention!" Then she blasts the funky hip-hop music over Planet Pom-Poms and the Honeys and the MayBees vibe out to the groove.

"It'll be a refresher, so try to pick up anything you missed or forgot from Monday's dance workshop."

I'm suddenly feeling nervous, but I grab Grammy's poms anyway. I fluff them carefully and then I hold them up to my nose. And right away, I feel better. Calmer. More focused, like I can do this.

The Stumbles move over and make room for me. Then LuLu turns to Brooklyn and says, "I never got the last part of the routine. Or the middle either. And, well, the beginning is kind of tricky, too."

"Don't worry," Brooklyn says coolly. "I memorized

the routine. And even though I look like a street breaker impersonating a cheer-popper, I can still help you through it if you want."

"Uh, yeah," LuLu says, her bob shaking back and forth. "I definitely want."

"Ignore my execution, just try to pick up the moves. I really have to learn how to be a softer dancer. I was always taught to hit the beats really hard with tons of force."

"Maybe try to be a little more ballet and a little less B-girl?" Winnie suggests.

Brooklyn chuckles to herself. "I always thought ballet was for wimps." She attempts a pirouette and awkwardly flails out of it. "Now I'd give anything to be more graceful and light on my feet."

"You'll get there," Winnie says. "We all will."

Gia and Yves pick up their poms and turn their backs to us to prep for the routine. They whiz through the tough choreography that involves a series of high kicks, a few grapevines, and several spins that transition into cool jumps. But when it's the Stumbles' turn to follow their lead, we all slam into one another after the first eight-count.

"Ooh, sorry," LuLu says as her poms fly out of her hands and swish through the air.

"No, that's my bad," Winnie says, rolling her chair straight into Lu. "Why do I keep turning the wrong way?"

"It's two turns to the right, then a high V into a lunge," Brooklyn explains.

"My brain knows that," Winnie groans, "but my body doesn't exactly agree with the choreography."

While Brooklyn helps Winnie and Lu, I turn to Cappie, who is hitting the steps perfectly.

"Cappie? What happens after the second grapevine to the left?" I ask, wrinkling my forehead.

"Why don't you ask Coach Brooklyn over there?" Cappie snarks, stomping her foot into the ground for emphasis.

"Sounds like somebody's jealous," Winnie whispers to LuLu.

Cappie pretends not to hear her and keeps dancing. But after a few grapevines, she sucks her teeth and decides to explain it to me after all. "Do the kick ball change and then step out on your left foot and heel turn."

"Ohhh, thank you!" I say, still totally confused, but happy that she's trying to help. "Like this?" I ask, showing her my sequence of mistakes.

"No! Your *other* left foot," she snaps before rolling her eyes. "I *just* said that."

"Hey, Magic," Brooklyn says to the beat of the music.

Then she models the moves for me in slow motion. "Step out this way. Then press your other heel down to turn."

I wring my hands in the air. "Let me try that again." And this time, I squeeze the handles on the poms and focus really hard on Brooklyn's directions. I can almost hear Grammy's voice in my ear: *You can do this, Magic.*

And when I try the sequence of steps again, I do it exactly like Brooklyn does and I end up on the beat with everyone else.

"That was purrrfect," LuLu sings as Winnie and Brooklyn shake their poms in the air for me.

I shake Grammy's poms back at them. "Thanks, B!"

"Let's all try it now," Brooklyn pipes up, clapping her poms to the beat. "Then go straight into the high kicks."

I try kicking my leg into the air but it doesn't move an inch past my hip.

"Magic," Brooklyn whisper-yells. "Before you lift your leg, bend both your knees to get some power under your kicks. It's a high-kick secret. We do it all the time in junior kickboxing."

"I think I can do that." I close my eyes and squeeze the handles of my poms again, hoping for another surge of help from Grammy Mae. I focus as hard as I can on bending my knees, and when I try again, I use the momentum to kick my leg high into the air. My foot flounders clumsily around my shoulder, but I'm definitely kicking better than before.

"That's it, Magic!" Brooklyn says. "Much better."

But Cappie doesn't seem to think so. And she doesn't waste any time letting me know.

"That's still not it." And then she kicks her leg to show me how it's done...and it whizzes past her forehead.

"Well, at least Magic is trying her best," Winnie snipes back at Cappie. She flips her strawberry curls and crosses her arms. "And if you're so good, why are you in our group anyway?"

Cappie eyeballs me, and then turns to walk away. She heads for the tree where our bags are hanging out, leaving me staring after her.

"Told you she's jealous," Winnie says, squinting at Cappie as she stalks away. "I'd recognize that green-eyed monster a mile away."

"What's there to be jealous about?" LuLu shrugs. "We're all in this together."

Winnie shakes her head. "I'm still not so sure that Cappie belongs with us. Something about her being in our group just doesn't feel right."

LuLu rubs her palms together. "Ooh, a real Stumble-Bees mystery."

For a second I wonder if Winnie is right. Could

Capricorn Reese really be jealous of the StumbleBees? But that seems ridiculous.

"It doesn't make sense to me. Why would she be jealous of Brooklyn? I mean, she's *Capricorn Reese*," I say, defending Cappie. "She was a Nickelodeon star." Then I turn and take off toward her.

"Let's be honest," Cappie says as I fall into step with her. She crosses her arms over her chest and smirks. "First it was Dallas and now it's Coach Brooklyn over there. You obviously don't want or need my help. I don't know why I'm even here—with the Stumbles, at camp. I feel like you don't even need me."

"But you're not…jealous, right?" I say under my breath. I'm trying to tread lightly because I'm not accusing Cappie—even though all signs point directly to the *J* word. "Brooklyn is just trying to help."

"Jealous? Of what? She's wasn't even doing it right."

"Then why didn't you show her how to do it?"

"Because I'm not here to babysit the Stumbles! I'm here to help *you*. Or at least I thought I was." She digs through her bag until she finds her reusable water bottle. Then she pulls it out and takes a long gulp of water and watches the Stumbles struggle through the next eight-count. "Why do you even want to be friends with them anyway?"

"Well," I say, looking at LuLu fumble over herself trying to nail the final leap-jump. And when she doesn't, she cracks up laughing with Winnie, whose wheels are stuck in the grass. "Because they're funny." And then Brooklyn takes them step-by-step through the next sequence. "And because they're nice."

"Well, go be with them, then. Your funny, nice, *new* friends." And then she says it. That thing that burns really bad in the pit of my belly. "Maybe *I* should just go find a new group of friends, too."

Then she walks away, and she looks every bit like a twelve-year-old green-eyed monster.

CHAPTER 15

The weather for Bonfire is perfect. It feels a little sticky. A little breezy. And the sky is neon blue with splashes of orange, purple, and some pink, too. The palm trees look like cool octopus arms blowing in the wind. And the air smells like ocean, but not like those scented candles that Mom always buys from Costco. It's summer beach weather at its best.

And I can't think of a better way to celebrate the end of our first week together at Planet Pom-Poms. I'm excited to see the actual bonfire—Fortune told me that when she summered at Planet Pom-Poms, it was one of her most memorable nights.

Cappie and I walk down the grassy lane that swerves in and out of the shrubs.

"This path leads to the beach," I keep telling her. "It opens up in a little bit and the view is *amazing*."

She doesn't bother to ask how I know. She just sighs heavily and then she goes, "Humph!"

I shrug and forge ahead anyway. She still hasn't gotten back to her old self since after yesterday's dance workshop. It's like she wants to pick a fight with me, but since we never really fight, she doesn't quite know how. So she just ignores me or keeps saying "Humph!" And I guess I don't say much either.

So we walk in silence until, just beyond the big tree, we spot it blazing: Twinkles of orange fire flicker through the air, making their way up to the sky. On an awesomeness scale from one to ten, I'd give it a nine. But the excitement in the air is already way past eleven.

"Hey, guys, over here!" Brooklyn yells to us as we kick our flip-flops into the air and catch them. It's the first thing we always do whenever our toes touch the sand. When we were little, neither of us could catch our flops on the first try. Usually we both giggle about it, but today, Cappie doesn't, so I don't either.

"We're over here!" LuLu giddy-screams at us.

I wave back to Brooklyn and the rest of StumbleBees.

They're hanging at the far end of the bonfire, just behind the MayBees.

"So glad you guys came," LuLu says, throwing her arms around me. When she tries to do the same to Cappie, Cappie takes a big step back and shakes her head.

"Absolutely not." She holds her hands up in front of her, like she's trying to fend off LuLu. "We're not doing that."

"She's not really a hugger," I try to explain.

"Okay," LuLu says, and shrugs with an apologetic smile.

"I'm so excited for tonight. I heard there's something *big* planned," Winnie says.

I stretch my neck to get a peek into the inner circle. That's when I spot Gia standing with the other Killer-Bees right in front of the fire. They're passing out marshmallows and graham crackers.

"They have chocolate, too," LuLu says. "But I don't think I should have any. My mom prefers broccoli florets over chocolate."

"Figures," says Winnie, swiveling her custom beach sand rider wheelchair around to face LuLu. "Your mom needs to learn that sometimes you just gotta let go and enjoy some good old-fashioned junk food."

"I don't do vegetables," I whisper to LuLu. "A girl has to draw the line somewhere." I reach into my hoodie pocket and pull out a Twizzler to offer her. She looks around, and then she takes it and smiles. When Winnie raises her eyebrows, I hand her one, too, and all is right in our circle. It only took smiles and candy—it was that simple.

"I love being at Planet Pom-Poms. I never thought being away from home would feel so safe." LuLu attempts a Herkie that she learned earlier in workshop. Sand flies everywhere. "I never want to leave," she says. "It's nice not having to hear my parents fighting at night when I'm trying to sleep."

Brooklyn puts her arm around LuLu's neck, but she has to bend all the way over to get cozy. She decides to rest her elbow on Lu's head instead, and both of them laugh.

"Can you believe it's already the end of our first week here?" I say.

"It went by so fast," LuLu agrees as she stares into the bonfire.

"Not fast enough," Cappie snaps, and her tone isn't nice, plain and simple. Her arms are folded over her chest like she's ready for a fight. My stomach clenches—I've seen her like this before, and it never leads to anything good.

Brooklyn's nose crinkles as she turns to Cappie. "Sounds like you don't want to be here."

Cappie huffs, and then she puffs.

"So why *are* you here?" Brooklyn presses harder.

"She doesn't mean to seem that way," I say quickly, trying to save the situation. "It's just that we're so busy learning and practicing and trying to remember everything that my head gets all foggy and I can't even think straight." I glance over at Cappie, praying for her to agree with me and smooth things over. "Right?"

"What she said," Cappie half answers, and stares out at the ocean.

"I feel that way too sometimes, like I can't even remember what day it is." I say, smiling at everyone to ease some of the tension and trying to move the conversation out of the danger zone. I really just want us all to get along—if Cappie gave the Stumbles a chance, I know she would see that there's no reason to be jealous of them. I don't want to lose my best friend, but I'm also making new friends for the first time since Cappie rang my doorbell in kindergarten and asked if I wanted to come outside and ride bikes.

"Yeah, me too," LuLu says, seeming to catch on to what I'm trying to do. "Wednesday took forever. We practiced for like four hours straight."

"For me it was Tuesday," Winnie adds. "Three hours in the sun nonstop."

Brooklyn shovels sand around with her toes. "It was Monday, Tuesday, *and* Wednesday for me." She glances up at Cappie and giggles. Brooklyn goes in for a high five, and Cappie halfheartedly fist-bumps her instead.

I exhale into my hoodie. *Whew.* It's a start.

"I'm nervous about MidSummer next weekend," Lu admits as one of the MayBees passes her a bag of marshmallows. "I hope I don't get cut."

"Parents. Fancy brunch. MidSummer cuts. Sounds *awesome,*" Winnie says, rolling her eyes.

Brooklyn and LuLu look at each other and snap, "Not!"

"I just don't feel like I'm getting better," LuLu admits. "My kicks are still super sucky. And so are my jumps. And my turns. And my splits. And my—"

"This stuff takes time." Brooklyn breaks it down for Lu. Then she turns to the rest of us. "*All* of our pirouettes are starting to get better. And so are our stunts and kicks and our dancing," she finishes, stopping the music at LuLu's pity party.

"I wish I was getting better, too," I say to the group.

"I think you're getting stronger for sure. Working out in the gym has really helped," Brooklyn encourages me. "You're gaining all that muscle memory."

"Her muscles don't have a memory, silly," says Lu.

"Of course they do, Lu," Winnie says. "Trust me, she's right, Magic. I always stand behind you in work-shop, so I've noticed."

"Why do you always stand behind *me*?"

"I like your socks. Supergirl and Wonder Woman are my jam. Plus I like the way you always do the robot dur-ing freestyle."

Something like pride swells in my chest. I can't believe someone other than Cappie would pay attention to me. I mean, the Poindexters are kind of required to, but the line pretty much stopped there. But now someone likes my socks, *and* likes my robot dance!

Then my attention shifts when I see, in the distance, some of the MayBees practicing their routine. And they're even better than the last time I saw them in workshop. The happy feeling in my chest deflates like a popped balloon.

LuLu stares at the MayBees, too, and pokes out her bottom lip. "I really need to amp up my practice time."

Brooklyn rubs her shoulder. "If you really want to, I'll keep working with you outside of workshop. And then, before you know it, you'll wake up in a few days and it'll have all come together."

Winnie rolls back and forth, accidentally shooting sand onto Cappie's toes. "And we'll all look so cute in our HoneyBee unis."

Cappie shakes her foot around and sand flies into the air. Then she growls at Winnie, "Well, if that's true, Winfrey, then why hasn't it happened for you?"

"That's why I'm here," Winnie retorts. "Fighting to make my dreams come true."

Brooklyn steps forward and crosses her arms. "You have to believe it to achieve it, Cappie. And we're *all* working toward our goals."

Cappie is not being the poster child for niceness. And we all scowl at her as she walks away.

"Is she always like that?" Winnie turns around to ask me. "Jealous?"

"And irritable?" Brooklyn adds.

"I've never seen her quite like this before." My eyes follow the dust trail my BFF is making toward the shoreline.

I stand up with a sigh. Time to get to the bottom of this. "I'll be right back."

Cappie is at the water's edge when I catch up to her. I open my mouth to ask her what's wrong right when Dallas Chase crosses our path. Our eyes lock and I lose all focus, my mouth opening and closing like a fish as I try to figure out what to say.

But then Gia saunters up to him and loops her arm through his before tossing her long ponytail over her shoulder at me. And then, just like that, he turns around and walks away with her.

Just. Like. That.

Cappie shakes her head at me before walking back to the bonfire. And I'm left standing at the shore. Alone.

I'm pretty sure this night can't get any worse: My best friend is slipping away from me, and if I'm being honest, watching Gia drape herself all over Dallas might sting even more. I think I want to go punch her in the face, which I've never felt before about anyone. And now I think my heart is beating dangerously fast. My grandpa takes medication for that. Maybe I need some, too.

I should just leave. Remove myself from the situation. And that's when I see Dallas say goodbye to Gia and wave to the other Killers before taking off with a double-marshmallowed s'more in his hand. Not even a whole second later, Gia turns around and looks in my exact direction. Then she smirk-faces me to death. I try to break eye contact with her, but I can't. It's only when the loud music blasts from the two speakers that her spell over me disappears. But now I'm in a whole other trance.

I see a group of girls in shiny purple-and-gold tracksuits running through a ponytailed mob of WannaBees. And the crowd goes wild when the girls tear off their sparkly jackets. They shriek even louder when one of them breaks into a rock star display of kicks, leap-jumps, and toe touches.

I run back to the Stumbles, my heart beating wildly in my chest. Could that be who I think it is?

"I don't think those are HoneyBees," Brooklyn says as I catch up to the Stumbles.

"Duh," Cappie says, standing on her tiptoes to get a better view. "Those are the Laker Girls."

"Ohmygosh!" LuLu says, jumping up and down. She grabs my arm and squeals into the air.

I jump up and down, too, but for a totally different reason. I'm peeking over the front line of shoulders in the mob of blond HoneyBee hair, squinting around to find Fortune. She has to be *somewhere* in the shimmery formation.

That's when I spy Cappie moving closer to the

dancers. When two of the Laker Girls notice her in the crowd, they start dancing with her. And when their formation changes, I see the girl in the front switch places with Fortune!

"She's here!" I yell to the StumbleBees. "Fortune's here!"

"That's your SIS-STAR?" LuLu asks as she dances around me.

Winnie rolls her chair closer to the mobile stage to get a better view. "But why is Cappie getting up there with the Laker Girls?"

I knock over a jumbo-sized bag of marshmallows to push through the clique of Honeys standing in front of the stage.

Winnie's right. Cappie's onstage with the superstar dancers and they're circling around her. She's caught in a dance trance, lost in the music, freestyling with them. And *everyone* is loving it. Even the Honeys are cheering for her.

And now my best friend feels miles away from the StumbleBees—and from me.

When the music finally stops, the Laker Girls smother her in hugs. And then when she comes down from the stage, the MayBees and even some of the Honeys flock to her, too. She's standing in front of the fire, soaking up all the attention like she just won a dance competition show. I look around for Coach Cassidy. Is she seeing this, too?

I finally spot her: She's standing on the other side of the bonfire, watching Cappie in all her glory. And I know in that very moment that Cappie won't be stuck as a StumbleBee much longer. Then our worlds will be pulled even further apart.

"Hey there, Pooh Bear," Fortune says, tickling me from behind. "Who's my favorite sissy?!" she tries again.

"Me," I say, sounding like a robot. I can't look away from Cappie and her crowd of admirers. "I am."

"And?"

"And God was having a good day when he made me," I blab, without my usual special sauce. Fortune pokes me in my rib cage and waits for me to burst into a gigglefest, but the Stumbles rush over and clobber her with attention before I do.

LuLu gushes, "You're the fabulous Fortune! Right here in the flesh!"

Winnie scoots past LuLu and offers her hand. "Hi. I'm Winfrey Walsh. You can call me Winnie. And it's a real pleasure to meet you."

"Well, hi there," Fortune says, wiping beads of sweat from her head. She checks out my new friends while she grabs her jacket and fans herself.

"And I'm Brooklyn, Magic's friend."

"I'm glad to meet you, too. All of you!" Fortune looks around. "But where's Cappie?"

I point to the fire and sigh. "Over there. With her new fans."

"Ohhh, so that explains the mood-i-tude." Fortune nods and strokes my check with the back of her hand. "Don't let that get to you, Sissy." Then she turns to the Stumbles. "Can I steal her away from you guys? Just for a little sister time. And when I'm done, how about a selfie session with each of you?"

The Stumbles nod in agreement and fumble around for their phones. Fortune holds up a finger and tells them, "Be right back" as she leads me down to the shore.

Fortune places her arm around my shoulder and pulls me close. "Why don't you tell me how camp has been going so far."

I shrug. "It's definitely had some ups and downs. But I'm still a total mess. And now Cappie's showed off all her skills and is going to be forced to leave the Stumbles."

"I seriously doubt she'd leave you in the group alone," Fortune says, shaking her head. "You've been here a whole *week*. And you've been learning and practicing every day, right?"

"Yeah, I have," I agree. Then when I think about it, I

add, "Sometimes twice a day. And I've even been going to the gym."

"But you always say the gym scares you! And that the machines look like Transformers." She tickles me in my side and before I know it, I'm doubling over in laughter.

"I guess they don't scare me anymore." I'm feeling so proud I could almost burst.

"See—overcoming your fears is just as important as learning the routines. And if you stick with it, you'll get stronger, and you know what strong muscles mean?"

"I'll be better at dance and at stunts," I offer as she nods at me. "That's what Coach and Brooklyn both say."

Fortune high-fives me and then she turns around to the eager Stumbles who are still standing along the edge of the bonfire waiting for her. They hold their phones in the air and wave them around. She waves back and then turns to face me.

"I like your new friends," Fortune says, chuckling. "Especially that Brooklyn."

"Yeah. Me too." I dig my toes into the sand and bury them. "But it's hard with Cappie not wanting to hang with us. I wish we could all be friends."

"She's not getting along with Brooklyn or Winnie or LuLu?"

"No. She doesn't really like them. Besides, it looks like she's already found a new group of friends." I can see Cappie chatting it up with some of the MayBees by the campfire. "That's what she said she was going to do."

"And how does that make you feel?"

I watch Cappie crunch down on her s'more with some of the other girls. Although part of me is happy that she's having fun at Bonfire, it still feels like she's slipping away. "It's just that I never imagined I'd lose my best friend."

"She has to have her own experience here at Planet Pom-Poms, and so do you," Fortune says kindly. "And if that means that you guys make new friends, that has to be okay, too."

I shrug. "I guess so. I just want us all to make the team."

Fortune winks at me. "If you keep working hard, anything is possible. Remember how Grammy Mae beat all the odds when she auditioned to become a Honey-Bee? She didn't look like the typical cheerleader on that court either. Before her, there were no Black cheerleaders at Valentine Middle. Just remember who you are, Sissy. You come from a long line of fierce, determined women." Fortune's smile is so wide it's almost blinding. "And now, it's your turn."

"Can I be honest?" I ask Fortune. She nods and leans in to listen closely. "Sometimes I don't feel so fierce."

"Whenever you start to doubt yourself, think about Grammy Mae's pom-poms to remind you of who you are and of where you come from."

"I will." I turn to look into my sister's eyes. "I miss home, too."

"I sure missed you guys when I was away, too. And you know there's never a dull moment in that house," she says, scrolling through her phone. She stops when she lands on a picture of Dad proudly holding a big bowl of soup in his hands. "Like last week, Mom was feeling a little under the weather. So Dad tried to make her famous homemade chicken noodle soup. But the chicken wasn't done and the noodles were overcooked and soggy."

"Ew!"

"I know. But can you believe that Mom actually ate it? She said she didn't want to hurt his feelings. She probably should've thrown it in the trash, because it ended up making her even sicker. Dr. Randall had to give her special medication for her stomachache."

"Poor Mom," I say when Fortune shows me a picture of her in bed making a sick face. "Is she feeling better?"

"Yeah. She was better the next day. But now she won't

let Dad anywhere near the stove." We laugh as she scrolls through her photos again, but this time she lands on a picture of a tiny black-and-white kitten. "And check out this little fur ball."

"Whoa! She's sooo cute! Where'd she come from?"

"We don't know. She just showed up at our front door the day you left for camp, so we started feeding her. Now she comes back every day like clockwork."

I can't help but clap my hands together feverishly. "Are we going to keep her?"

"Mom said we can feed her as long as she keeps coming around." Then Fortune shows me three more cute shots of the kitty before flipping through more photos of the Poindexters. I take the phone out of her hands, barely able to stop grinning, and then play a video of Mom and Dad having a dance-off after movie night, even though Dad can't dance to save his life. All he knows how to do is a basic two-step from side to side. So Mom always wins the weekly contest, and Dad has to give her a foot massage.

"Thanks, Fortune," I say, passing the phone back to her. "For coming to see me and for giving me the deets on the Poindexters. Even though I'm not there, it makes me feel closer to home."

"Well, you and I both know the Poindexters never

disappoint. And, Sissy, really, where else would I be?" she asks, kissing my forehead. "Now, you've got some serious business to take care of while you're here. So stay focused and stay—"

"Fierce and determined—just like Grammy Mae," I say, grinning.

"That's right, Sissy." She ruffles my hair. "Just like Grammy Mae."

CHAPTER 16

Last night's heavy conversation with Fortune left me craving a big dose of comfort food. So the next morning I pad over to my candy stash in my middle drawer and that's when I see the note Cappie scribbled for me. It's taped to the mirror above my mouthwash:

> Needed to get started early.
> See you out there.

See you out there?

I slide down the wall and bury my head between my knees. But then after a few seconds of pouting, I decide to handle this maturely. Instead of obsessing over Cappie's choices, I'm going to make some big-girl choices of my own. So I take the liberty of borrowing her curling wand to tackle my hair. Decided: Not only am I going to act more mature, I'm going to look it, too.

Fortune used to have a sparkly vanity in her room and I'd sit cross-legged on her bed and watch her as she got ready in the morning. So I grip the wand and take clumps of my hair at a time, smoothing them around the barrel, just like I've seen her do. It seemed to take her forever to get each curl just right, but it was always worth it. I don't have that kind of time today, so I jumble all my hair around the grooves of the wand one last time and spritz it all in place.

Then I apply some shimmery makeup around my eyes. I swivel the brush around the purple eye shadow and swipe it across my eyelids a few times. When I'm done, I take a step back and survey the new and improved me. For some reason, I don't look as polished as Fortune always did. In fact, I look more like a cross between a raccoon and a clown.

I decide to wipe off some of the face paint and keep the rest. Then I grab two giant fistfuls of Kleenex and stuff my training bra, smushing my baby boobs to the center of my chest. It isn't exactly a secret that I'm the vice president of the famous itty-bitty committee. And even though the tissue is making my bra lumpy, I'm already feeling more mature and HoneyBee-ready.

I nod to myself in the mirror and race out the door to the sandy volleyball court.

I fly through the Daffodil Field, trying to hold my hair together. Coach told us that she was so impressed with how hard we've been working that she was rewarding us with a volleyball game as a change from our normal practice routines. I'm thrilled to have a break from practice, but I'm even more pumped for everyone to see the new, improved me.

The volleyball court is in the middle of a big rectangular sand lot surrounded by grass that had been plopped right between the football field and the dorms.

I'm feeling pretty confident as I prance over to Cappie, who's standing coolly next to the net waiting for her turn to get in the game. Brooklyn, LuLu, and Winnie are just a few steps behind her. Some of the MayBees are on one side of the net and a handful of Honeys are on the other, including Gia and Yves. It's now or never. I can feel the butterflies flitting around in my belly when I tap Cappie on her shoulder. I guess I have a lot riding on this moment. Hopefully, she'll think I'm just as cool and grown-up as her new friends. But when she turns around, instead of applauding, she shrieks. And the Killer-Bees stop the game to point and laugh, too.

"She looks like a raccoon!" Gia declares from across the court.

"Yeah, 1980 called and they want their look back," another girl rants from the net.

"You're right, G, she really is Tragic!" Yves teases. "Total Tragic Magic."

I want to run. I should probably run. I'm *definitely* going to run.

But when I turn to do so, Brooklyn and LuLu come after me.

"Magic, wait!" Brooklyn yells, catching up. "Hold on a sec."

I look past them and see the HoneyBees giggling, anxiously waiting to see what I'll do next. In the distance, I spy Coach fussing at them for teasing me. I overhear the words "juvenile" and "childish" sizzle through the air.

"What do you think you're doing? She's a prospect, just like you," Coach fumes, scrolling through her iPad. "And this is not sportsmanlike. I'm deducting points for everyone who made fun of her."

LuLu tugs on my shoulder. "I think you look kinda rad. Definitely like an eighties throwback with the glittery eyes." She fusses with my hair. "And this mane is something special."

"But I wasn't exactly going for an eighties vibe," I groan.

Lu pulls me over to the other StumbleBees. "Yeah, but it's here now. So just go with it."

Winnie giggles anyway. I cringe as she wheels her chair around me in circles to get a closer look. "That's quite a look. What were you thinking?"

"I dunno." I blink back tears. "I guess I—"

"She *wasn't* thinking," Cappie snarls, and pulls me to the side. "What're you doing? You look like a clown."

"I keep telling you guys that retro is cycling back in a major way. That's what my Fab Girl Insta feed says. So, see, you're right on trend." LuLu whips out her compact to show me.

Despite the Stumbles fashion report, Cappie is right. I do look like I stood in the middle of the street with a giant metal umbrella during a lightning storm. Half my hair is frizzed out and brittle, while the other half is flat and fried.

Then the Stumbles start pulling their hair out of their ponytail holders and messing theirs up, too. LuLu takes out one of her colored lip glosses and smears it all over her eyelids. "I'm telling you, cycling back in a may-jah way."

Soon, Brooklyn and Winnie join in and cover their cheeks and lips in sticky pink lip gloss, too. It isn't long before we're all laughing so hard we can barely stand until I let out a snort. Then we just laugh harder.

"Stupid Stumbles," Cappie says under her breath as she walks away to talk to one of the MayBees with piercing blue eyes and a dark pixie haircut named Claire.

Coach isn't impressed with our throwback fashion. "Let's get back to our game, girls." Her whistle dangles from her neck and she massages her forehead. "The score is tied. Green team, it's your turn to serve."

The game drags on for the entire morning. But when Coach asks to talk to Cappie, everything in my world stops. The Stumbles and I don't waste any time eavesdropping.

"Cappie, I want to talk to you about your dancing," Coach says.

Cappie looks over her shoulder and glances at me. My legs and arms stiffen, mainly because I have a good idea about what's about to happen.

"I've been watching you this past week and it seems that you're much more advanced than I thought you were at diagnostics."

We all lean in a little closer and hear Coach say, "And last night at Bonfire, your freestyle looked really polished and competitive. I'm thinking that you'd be a better fit with the green group instead of the yellow."

Cappie nods and then looks over Coach's shoulder to where Claire is standing and watching her. And then . . . she . . . *smiles*. She doesn't even bother to check in with me about this terrifying group change.

We'd agreed that she'd stay with me all through camp, right where a BFF is supposed to be. But Fortune was right last night: Things *are* going to change. I just didn't know it would happen this fast or feel this crushing.

Coach puts her hand on Cappie's shoulder and asks, "How does that sound to you?"

"Actually, I think that's a good idea," Cappie says, finally turning around to face me and the Stumbles. "It's been a while since I've danced, and I guess I'm not as rusty as I thought I was. The green group sounds more my speed."

"Great," Coach says, and turns to walk back toward the court. "You're a really good dancer with tons of competitive edge. And if my gut is right, I think you've got exactly what it takes to help the Honeys win another title."

Cappie grins, and I feel my stomach drop. This can*not* be happening.

LuLu's eyes are wide. "So Cappie's out of our group?"

"Sure looks that way," Brooklyn confirms as Cappie walks back to the net to join Claire in the sand.

But I can't let it go, not without an explanation. I take a deep breath and walk right up to Cappie, tugging her arm to pull her away from her new group mates.

"Wh-what just happened, Capp?" I whisper.

"I think you guys eavesdropped enough to hear." Then she shrugs. "I'm one of the green girls now."

"But why would you agree to be a MayBee? I thought you were going to be a StumbleBee with me?"

Cappie scoffs. "You've got the Stumbles now. You don't need me anymore. And it sure doesn't feel like you *want* me either."

I scrunch my brows and shake my head. I can't imagine not needing or wanting Capricorn Reese in my world. "How can you say that?"

"It's clear that I don't belong with the Stumbles."

"But you haven't even *tried*," I plead.

"They're just not my jam, Magic. And if we're both being honest here, it seems like you like them more than me anyway."

"But it's not the same. They're different from you, but that doesn't mean I like them *more*."

"You're working out with Brooklyn and not me. And you make dumb jokes with them that I don't even think are funny." Then she points to my face in serious disapproval. "And your clown face and hair even match theirs now."

"But Cappie, you hate the gym," I say, trying hard to explain. "And they're so funny. I can't believe you don't think they're funny, too," I say. "And you would never walk around camp with your face and hair like this."

"That's exactly my point." Then she says something that I can't compete with no matter how much I try. "And I want to dance again, Magic. I mean *really* dance, not fake-dance like I was doing when I was trying to dumb it down to keep up with you."

And at this very moment, my whole body feels like it's sinking into an ocean of quicksand and I'm struggling to keep afloat.

"Since I've been here," Cappie continues, "I've realized that I miss being onstage. I miss performing."

"But you never even wanted to be a HoneyBee," I say, holding back tears. "You think they're stupid."

"Well, some of them seem cool...from what I can tell. And Claire and some of the other MayBees are cool, too."

In one last attempt to keep my friend from abandoning me, I do my half of the Reptile handshake.

But Claire yells, waving over to her. "Cappie! It's our turn to play. Come on!"

And Cappie runs toward her, not even looking back at me.

And I'm left hanging as I try to breathe, but I'm only sinking deeper into that quicksand.

CHAPTER 17

Still in shock over losing my best friend to the May-Bees, I chomp down on a Twizzler and sulk over to the gym. I'm supposed to meet Brooklyn for a workout sesh, but I'm feeling utterly defeated. So instead I sit on the curb outside the gym and watch the squirrels run up and down the tree in front of me.

"Hey, Magic!"

My belly lurches when I look up to see Dallas Chase walking through the gym doors.

"Hi," I say, looking away, mainly because I don't know what else to do. I mean, I'm completely caught off guard here. And I haven't actually talked to him since I was barfing under the stars on the beach.

"What're you doing here?" he asks, like we just hung out yesterday.

"Uh...working out." Then I consider that I'm sitting on my butt stalking the squirrels. "I mean...I'm here to work out. With Brooklyn." I nod and sway back and forth on my tailbone. He sits down next to me and does the same thing.

"Sooo...did you hear about Logan getting bit by a snake?"

My jaw drops. "You mean the kid you told me about? The one who got so good last summer that he became the star receiver?"

"Yeah, but he wasn't exactly feeling like a football jock when he thought his ear was going to fall off. It was so funny. He kept running in circles, screaming and holding his earlobe."

Then he starts imitating Logan, and I laugh so hard I almost choke on my candy. Before I know it, we're laughing our faces off like we actually did just see each other yesterday. Being with him is so easy, like being with Cappie used to be.

After we finally catch our breath, we sit around

watching the squirrels fight for the leftover sandwich hanging out next to the trash can. Then out of nowhere, he asks, "What's it like growing up with a famous dad?"

"Well," I say, thinking about it. "Sometimes it can be fun. Like going to Disneyland every summer with VIP passes to the theme parks. He gets the whole family together, so my cousins, my aunts, and my uncles join us, too. He calls it Poindexter Day."

"Sounds like a good time. You're pretty lucky, you know."

"I guess," I say, but then I decide to be brutally honest. "Except those days when it isn't a good time."

"What's not to love?" he asks. "I'm sure you get court-side seats to all the sports games."

"Yeah," I say, fidgeting with my shoelaces. "But sometimes I don't exactly fit in with the rest of my family."

"What do you mean? You *are* a Poindexter, right?"

"Of course I am. But not everyone thinks I am. Like, when we're taking pictures or on the red carpet for some fancy event, I usually get asked to stand off to the side while they take the family photos."

"Why would anyone do that?"

"Because the red carpet lady never thinks I'm part of my own family. And it gets really annoying. My parents have to always make sure they know I'm a Poindexter, too. I might as well just wear a name tag. At a movie premiere last month, the photographer literally *shoved* me out of the way."

"Did your dad punch him?" Dallas balls his fist and punches at the air. "That's what I would have done."

"Of course not." I twist my face into a frown. "If he punched everyone who pushed me to the side, he'd be in really big trouble."

Dallas takes a second to consider that before turning to me to say, "I want to tell you something, too."

"What do you want to tell me?" I ask, shrugging. I feel like we've already talked about everything I'd write in my diary. "What's up?"

"I just want you to know that there's a reason I wanted to hang out with you and train you." He looks down at his fingers that are looping the drawstring into a bow on his practice shorts.

"Yeah? I thought that maybe you felt sorry for me, so you made me your summer project: *The Biggest Loser: Middle School Edition.*"

He jabs me in the shoulder. "Wow. That's really what you think of me?"

"Well...I'm sort of a geekster, and you're one of the cool kids—all popular and superhero-ey. You've got fans and followers, and well, I *definitely* don't."

"I'm really not as cool as everyone makes me out to be."

"From where I'm standing, you are. Which is why I'm guessing you don't talk to me when you see me in public."

I watch his face turn a shade of fire-engine red. And I wonder if I shouldn't have said that. But then I realize: *Wait a minute; I deserve answers.*

"I know you see me at the café. And at practice. And at Bonfire." I can hear my voice shaking, but that doesn't stop me from forging ahead anyway. "Are you ashamed of me?"

"No!" he says, shifting his brows around as he shakes his head. "That's definitely not it."

"Then why do you ignore me?" I feel really bad all of a sudden—and invisible, just like on the red carpet. I tap my foot on the steps. "I'm listening."

"This is where it gets complicated. I mean," he starts, and then he looks away. But after taking a long pause, he exhales and finishes, "I guess you could say I'm scared of being teased and made fun of."

"Who would make fun of you? You're *Dallas Chase.*" I laugh, but it sounds a little hollow. "Even Tragic Magic can't ruin Dallas Chase."

He exhales heavily. "I wasn't always this version of

me. I guess you could say I changed when I moved to Santa Monica. But before that, I was teased a lot and bullied, too. So I know how that feels. And I don't want the kids in the cool world, as you call it, to treat me that way again." He pauses. "I'm sorry I've been such a jerk."

I stop and take in everything he just said. "But you're so...perfect."

"I'm far from perfect, Magic. There's so much more to me than what you see."

No one at school had ever really questioned Dallas's total, supreme awesomeness. He'd just arrived one day and changed the face of Valentine Middle to one with dirty-blond hair and dreamy green eyes. I couldn't imagine him being anything other than Boy Wonder, action hero in training. But I guess it could be true. Stranger things have happened. I mean, look at me, auditioning to be a HoneyBee.

I shake my head at him. "I can't believe that anyone would ever tease you!"

"Well, they did. And it didn't feel good. That's one of the reasons I want to help you. Some stuff about you reminds me of...me."

"Then why don't you talk to me when you see me or come hang out with me? Especially since you say you understand. And, by the way, my new friends would never bully you; they're pretty cool," I boast, very matter-of-fact. But then I sigh, because for the first time, I don't feel sorry for *me*, I actually feel sorry for *him*.

"I'm hanging with you now, watching the squirrels," he points out.

"You're not afraid of what kids might say anymore?"

"Honestly, Magic, this has been the best conversation I've had since I've been at camp." I watch him rub the back of his neck and half smile at me. "Now, can I ask you something that's been on my mind?"

"Go ahead. Shoot."

"Why didn't you ever come back down to the beach to work out with me again?"

I give this question some serious thought and then I shrug. "I guess that's complicated, too," I admit, chuckling at the irony. "If I'm being honest, I didn't want Cappie or Gia and her friends to get mad at me. I definitely didn't want to give your girl more ammunition to kill me."

"Gia? Well, first, she's not exactly my girl. We just hang out. And second, she wouldn't kill you."

"You're right, she'd just sting me to death." I shudder at the thought of it before revealing more of my confusion. "I don't get why you even hang out with her. She isn't exactly the nicest Bee in that hive."

"You wouldn't understand."

166

"That's complicated, too?" I cross my arms over my chest. "Well, try me."

"It's just that I'm *supposed* to hang out with her. She's the head cheerleader and I'm the star quarterback. It's like everyone expects us to be an *item*—or whatever."

"But she's not a nice person. She's actually kinda mean. And you're, well, you could really be awesome."

"You really think I could be awesome?"

I pat him on the back without answering, but I send up a wish for him to find real friends. The kind that will encourage him to be who he really is and make sure he feels good about it. I wish he finds friends like the Stumbles.

But he can't have them because they're already taken.

CHAPTER 18

Dallas and I finish naming the family of squirrels running around the big tree in the distance just as Brooklyn pokes her head out of the gym's double doors.

"Hey, Magic! There you are," Brooklyn says as her eyeballs shoot back and forth between Dallas and me. "Are we doing this workout thing or not?"

Dallas stands up and stretches. "I gotta jet anyway." He heads toward the football field, but then he pivots back to me and nods. "I guess it wasn't as complicated as I thought, after all."

I wave as he jogs away. Then I get up and dust myself

off before following Brooklyn into the gym. "I'm all yours."

And to my surprise, she doesn't ask any questions about Dallas; instead, she just says, "I'm so glad you came."

We speed down the hallway and turn the corner, bumping right into Coach. She's leaning against the water fountain with her iPad in her hands. And after she checks in with us about what exercises we'll be doing, we head over to the mats next to the trainers.

"We'll go easy today," Brooklyn says, "especially since we have stunt practice this afternoon. Plus I know you're sore. Just try to breathe through it."

"'Kay," I say, and sit on the mat next to her. Then I spread my legs as far apart as they can possibly go.

She starts with those same offensive stretches that I hate every time we're here. I watch her breathe in and out slowly. "Dad always tells me to inhale effort, exhale pain. He calls that a master stretch."

My head is between my legs, trying to touch the mat as my hamstrings stretch like a worn-in ponytail holder.

"You're really looking good. This is your best stretch so far." She high-fives me and I press my head even closer to the mat. "Let's switch it up and head to the track today to start our workout," she says, tugging at my wrist. "We'll begin with suicide runs."

"Why does that have to sound like death?"

"I don't know. I never really thought about it, but you're right. Let's call them easy empowerment runs instead."

Changing the name of the exercise didn't make it any less deadly. We run up and down the track until my hips are ready to pop out of their sockets. Brooklyn's idea of "easy" means endless empowerment runs and infinite reps of crunches (which, by the way, only make me think of Cap'n Crunch, the kind with the berries, and then I'm hungry all over again. And I'm pretty sure that's not the point of all this).

"You know, you're doing much better," she says, bending over to catch her breath. "And I know you always say you can't dance or stunt or flip, but you've been improving faster than anyone here during practice. I mean, your execution needs work, but the foundation is there. And it's looking pretty dope."

I wipe the sweat from my brow and massage my calves. "*You* think *I'm* dope?"

"Duh!" she says, shoving into me. "And with more practice, you could really have a shot at making the team."

"I hope you're right, B. But there's no way I want to do it without the Stumbles. I'm so glad I met you guys,"

I confess. Then I lower my voice like I'm about to tell her the biggest secret ever. "In case you hadn't guessed, I don't exactly have very many friends."

"Neither do I," she says, after giving it some thought. "But at least you've got Cappie and . . . Dallas?"

"I wouldn't call him my *friend*. But he is interesting, to say the least." And that's all I say about Dallas Chase—Boy Wonder—because he trusted me with another secret, and I plan on protecting it.

"I guess I don't really have time for friends," Brooklyn admits, finishing her last crunch. "When I'm not studying for school or at a Scout meeting or practicing my dance moves, then I'm helping my dad with work."

I start counting on my fingers. "Let's see, I have you guys. And then there's Cappie—maybe. That's kind of up in the air right now."

"Do you think Winnie was right about her being jealous of us?"

I bite my lip. "Sometimes I think so, but that's still hard for me to believe. I've never seen her *this* bad before."

"Have you ever made new friends since you two have been tight?"

I shake my head at the thought. "Not until I met you guys. And now it just feels like she's gone."

Brooklyn rubs her chin and then she says, "Losing a

friend is a lot like losing someone in your family. Everything changes because they're not there anymore, at least not like they used to be."

"Like my Grammy Mae."

"Were you two close?"

"Yeah, she was my favorite human alive. She was always nice to me and she made me feel like I mattered, like she saw me, you know, for who I *really* am, not just what everyone expected me to be. I wish she could see me now. She always wanted me to try and be a HoneyBee."

Brooklyn puts her hand over her heart and exhales loud enough for both of us. "She sounds really special, Magic."

I nod back at her. "We were a lot alike. She even stood on her tiptoes when she washed the dishes like me."

Brooklyn smiles when I say that. Then she asks softly, "How did you deal with losing her?"

"I don't think I did such a good job," I say. "Most of the time, it felt like I couldn't breathe. And then sometimes my heart would race, and it seemed like the walls were going to smother me. But the crying was the toughest part. Sometimes I'd be in class and I'd be sobbing, and I wouldn't even realize it."

"Wow, Magic." Brooklyn sighs. "I know exactly how that feels."

"Aw, man, B. I'm so sorry." I lay my hand on her shoulder. "Here I am going on and on about my grammy and you're still trying to deal with the loss of your mom. I didn't mean to be insensitive and—"

"Don't worry," she says, smiling through her discomfort. "You weren't being insensitive at all. It's nice to talk to someone who's lost someone. You were lucky to have her. And you're lucky to still have your mom, too."

"You can always borrow her," I say, grabbing her hand. "I'm happy to share."

"I just might take you up on that," she says, leading me past the climbing wall, toward the Transformers on the other side of the gym. "See, I told you . . . that's something that only a true friend would do."

She motions for me to hop on the machine with the handlebars and I start my first set of arm curls with no problem. "Are you okay?"

"Sometimes . . . ," she begins, nodding for me to start the next set. "Sometimes I don't have any thoughts in my head about her at all. And then other times, I have all these thoughts at the same time. That's when my heart starts beating fast and my hands get all clammy and I can't catch my breath."

"Because you have too many thoughts?"

"It's just that . . . what if one day I wake up and I can't

remember her? Sometimes," she says, looking at the floor, "I get really down. And I'm scared that I won't remember the way she smelled or the way she smiled."

And I totally understand that, because even though I've never met her mom before, I don't want her to forget her mom either. I reach for her hand and put mine on top of hers.

"My dad thinks I should talk to someone about it, like a therapist. Or a counselor for kids or something. But... I dunno. I've never really talked to anybody about this stuff before." Then she looks at me and we both know what she means. "Well, not before you."

"I'll go with you if you want," I say. Talking to people can be scary, and I know I'd want someone with me if I were doing something that brave.

"You'd really do that?"

"Sure! You've been here for me." I flex my arm muscle and we both see that something is starting to form there. We grin at each other.

"You know, I think I'd like that."

"Me too," I say, and throw my arm around her shoulder. "Me too."

And just like that, I sink into a smile because I know without a doubt that this is how true friendship is supposed to feel.

CHAPTER 19

A few days later, Planet Pom-Poms is totally transformed.

The entire Great Lawn is now one humongous Honey-Bee Carnival with a monster Ferris wheel in the center of it all. The carousel and bounce house are right next to it, and the lines are already wrapped around the face painter and the funnel cake stand. I even heard that a petting zoo has been set up in the Daffodil Field. But when me and Brooklyn try to make our way out of the maze to meet up with the other Stumbles, we keep hitting dead ends.

"Are you okay?" Brooklyn asks, looping her arm

through mine. We're nearing the end of the second week at camp and I'm dreading the fact that MidSummer is only a few days away.

"Yeah," I lie as we find the exit and catch up to the Stumbles.

"It's totally okay if you're not okay, ya know," Brooklyn says, leading the way past the corn dogs. And that's when we all spot her: Cappie!

We watch Claire pull Cappie into the beanbag toss line.

Winnie rolls her chair back and forth before stopping. Then she hands each of us a big swirl of blue-and-pink cotton candy. "They were partners for the wheelbarrow race, too."

The shiny Honeys take turns throwing the beanbag pouches into the holes. When Cappie steps up, they scream for her like she's about to save the planet from a rival zombie cheerleader attack.

Everything is so different now. Just a few days ago they were laughing at Cappie and making fun of her, but now they won't even leave her side to get popcorn. They're the new definition of sucking up. And it's majorly gross.

"It was only a matter of time, I guess," LuLu says, twisting her tongue around the sticky candy. "I'm sure she missed the spotlight. I mean, she was a Nickelodeon baby, after all. And I heard from my next-door neighbor's cousin that they're given some kinda celebrity card for life." She swallows hard and stares at Winnie as she opens her third bag of Flamin' Hot Cheetos. "They can just snap their fingers, and they instantly have fame again." Then LuLu shoves her nose in the Flamin' Hot Cheetos bag and inhales. She comes up for air wearing a weird smile with blood-orange dust stuck to the tip of her nose.

LuLu turns to Brooklyn and asks, "Does that fame card come with rehab? 'Cuz most of these child stars grow up to—"

"To get pulled over by the police after joyriding through Hollywood in a stolen golf cart," Winnie finishes.

Everyone recalls Caleb Rhiner. He was the star from that kids' show *Caleb for President*. He stole a golf cart from the set and was found on Melrose Avenue after he crashed into a row of parking meters. He was thirteen and "a really bad seed," according to most of the adults who were talking about him last month at the Chipotle on Main Street.

Brooklyn shakes her head before moving on. "Now, who's going on the Ferris wheel with me?"

"I'm afraid of heights," LuLu admits.

"How are you going to be our flyer in practice? We have to work on our stunts for MidSummer," says Brooklyn.

LuLu flips her bob around to me and asks, "Do you really think Cappie's going to steal a golf cart and go to kiddie jail?"

Brooklyn spins around. "I don't think that's what she meant. She's just saying that being a child starlet does something to you. And for Cappie, it's caused a severe addiction to the limelight."

"And I hear that's a pretty serious addiction," says Winnie, turning the bag of chips upside down to suck out all the crumbs.

"Worse than Flamin' Hot Cheetos?" Brooklyn eyes Winnie's glowy fingertips as she opens her fourth bag.

We all giggle. Poor Winnie. She couldn't keep her promise to us to abstain from Flamin' Hot Cheetos for more than six hours. I'm probably the only one who completely understands. I look around and bite off the head of a new Twizzler.

"Don't worry, Magic. You've got us now." Brooklyn sweetens the moment.

"Yeah," says Lu. "And we don't have an addiction to the limes."

"Limelight," Winnie repeats, sucking her fingertips clean.

"I know. That's what I said," Lu huffs. "I don't even like limes."

"I'm more of a lemon girl myself." Brooklyn joins Lu's train of thought, ignoring the epic eye roll Winnie is sending their way.

When I spot Dallas in the crowd, next to the photo booth, I catch a case of tunnel vision and the Stumbles become instant background noise. Dallas is casually leaning against the booth, popping kernels of popcorn into his mouth, two at a time. He's perfection in his faded Valentine tee and distressed, triple-wash jeans. Then it happens: He turns to me and we lock eyes. I know because I can't bring myself to look away. And neither does he, even though there's a bunch of bouncing heads in the space between us. But then he waves. And I hurry to wave back. And I can't stop waving— that is, until Gia pops up. Perfect timing. And of course, she follows his gaze and sees...me. *That's* when he looks away.

I shift my weight around awkwardly. But I continue to stand there—and stare. That's when she ruffles his hair and I can feel my legs turning to limp taffy. And yes, I'm still staring. I honestly can't look away. Especially now. It's like when somebody vomits all over the floor. *Ew.* It's nasty and foul, but you still stare anyway. And Gia makes sure I see every second of it. *Double ew!*

"Magic, what do you think?" I hear Brooklyn ask.

"About what?" I turn to the Stumbles.

"Weren't you listening?" Winnie pushes.

"Sorry," I say, and turn back to Gia and Dallas. "What's the question?"

Gia pulls Dallas into the photo booth and I feel like I'm the booth's security guard the way my eyes are now glued to it. The red velvet curtain flaps in the wind when Gia abruptly closes it. I fear the worst is happening. *What if they're turning the photo booth into a* kissing *booth?*

"Winnie is worried about not advancing past Mid-Summer."

"Why on earth is she worried?" I ask, annoyed at the events I imagine are unfolding in that booth.

"The obvious," Winnie says. "I'm not exactly moving around like everyone else over here."

"But is that a bad thing?" I turn my full attention back to the Stumbles because when one of them needs help, nothing else matters. "Listen, Winn, the HoneyBees need to be shaken up. And I think you're just the one to do it."

LuLu's head bobs up and down as she nods in agreement. "Yeah, what she said."

"All the stunts and chair tricks you've learned are super sick," Brooklyn says.

"With all of our differences," I continue, "we're like a cool bag of Skittles. Each of us has our own unique flavor. Without one of us, the rest of the bag would be boring." I smile at the thought of a bag of Skittles. "And Winnie, you're the green one."

"Look, Magic's tongue is purple," Brooklyn says, pointing at what's left of my cotton candy.

I stick my tongue out and see that she's right. "And yours is green."

That's when Winnie and Lu stick their orange and blue tongues out, too.

Brooklyn laughs so hard she doubles over. "It's a StumbleBee rainbow."

But I immediately stop laughing when Gia and Dallas finally come out of the photo booth. Good thing, too, because I was wondering if I was going to have to charge in and rescue them. I mean, what if their lips had gotten stuck together?

Dallas's cheeks are fire-engine red, and Gia's lips are puckered as she reapplies her lip gloss.

Yuck!

"So what're we doing next?" They all turn to me and wait for an answer, but I don't have one. I'm still reeling from the sight of Gia and Dallas, who I watch until they disappear into the crowd with Yves and Logan somewhere over by the karaoke machine.

"I was going to ask you to go on the Ferris wheel with me," LuLu says to Brooklyn.

Brooklyn's brow furrows. "But I thought you were afraid."

"I was," she admits, looking down at Winnie. "But since we're all taking chances," she says, and skips toward the Ferris wheel. Brooklyn howls into the air and skips off behind her.

I lean down and squeeze Winnie's shoulder. "You good?"

"Yeah!" she says, popping her chair into a wheelie and then rocking her chair from side to side on each wheel in a circle around us. "You like that crabwalk?"

"Pretty fresh, Winn," I tell her, glad to see she's back to her old self.

And then she looks up at me and we fist-bump into

StumbleBee happiness. And things are back to normal. Just the way they're supposed to be.

"I think I just lost my head!" I scream at Brooklyn as my ponytail flies around in the air. "Is it still attached to my body?"

"I'm going to lose my caramel apple if this thing doesn't stop," she warns from across the seat of the Tilt-A-Whirl. Her face turns blue and she grabs her belly. "Whose bright idea was this anyway?"

Winnie throws her hands into the air and screams, "I lovvve it!" And then when our chair spins around and around, LuLu slides into her side and she laughs even harder. "That tickles!"

Winnie explained that the Tilt-A-Whirl was her absolute fave ride at carnivals because it was one of the only ones she was allowed to experience. We were so excited to go on it with her as we helped her onto the ride, and we all made sure she was secure between us when the ride started, with the bar pulled down over our laps. But now that we're tilting and whirling, maybe *Brooklyn* should have been the one to reconsider getting on it.

"Make this thing stop!" Brooklyn screams into the air.

We all try not to laugh but it's so hard because her eyes keep rolling around in her head every time the car tilts and spins.

When the ride is finally over, Brooklyn stumbles to the exit. "That was torture."

"Are you really going to puke?" I ask her. "Because I can hold your headphones."

"Nah. I'm good now that I'm back on solid ground."

"So...no churros for you?" Winnie asks as the ride attendant helps her back into her chair. She unlocks her brakes and points to the churros man in the red-and-white-striped suit. "That's my next stop. C'mon!" We follow Winnie's lead through the grass right up to the sweet treats. "Churros for everyone!" she yells to the man at the cart.

I take one and so does Lu. But Brooklyn turns her nose up and fake-vomits. "I'm good." Then she glances at her watch. "Guys! Magic's going to miss her call time."

"I'm supposed to be interviewed at three thirty," I say, forcing myself to think about what I'm going to say. *Yikes!* All the WannaBees are being interviewed today for our MidSummer auditions. Coach explained that our individual videos will play after she introduces us when we take the stage.

"Are you ready for your close-up?" LuLu says,

shaping her hands into a pretend movie camera and pointing them at each of us.

"Is it time already?" Winnie asks, and then swivels her chair around us. "I'm supposed to be there at four."

LuLu checks her phone. "I'm at four fifteen."

"My call time is three forty-five," Brooklyn says as she pop-locks around me. "So it's almost time for me to get my shine on."

Winnie dusts the sugar off her fingertips and then twirls her strawberry curls around her fingers until they're perfectly spiraled. "I'm ready."

"I love being in front of the camera," Brooklyn admits, while Lu and Winnie continue primping.

Apparently, everyone is excited about this—everyone except me! Just being in front of a camera phone still spooks me, even more than Halloween Horror Nights. This whole lights-camera-action thing was something Fortune failed to mention when she gave me the rundown on MidSummer.

"It's 3:29!" Brooklyn panics, turning to me.

"Coach said we can't be late," Winnie says, and then starts power-rolling toward the pink-and-gold tent with the HOLLYWOOD sign on top of it.

"Magic, run!" Winnie orders. "And don't be scared. We're right behind you."

"Yeah, we'll meet you there." LuLu nods, and then they all nod along with her.

I sprint down to the end of the Great Lawn and am completely winded when I pull back the tent flap and step inside.

Whoa. It's like a mini movie studio set. There are cameras everywhere with lights all over the place. People are standing around with clipboards and earpieces and right in the middle of it all is a long green screen with a single chair in front. And Cappie is sitting in it.

"You must be Magic," one of the clipboard holders says. "Come over here so we can get you mic'd up."

But I'm stuck watching Cappie answer the interview questions like a real-life superstar. She tosses her hair over her shoulder and sweet-laughs into the camera. "I've been dancing since I was three. I did TV for a while and even had a part in a movie, but in the end, there's nothing like dancing. So, I guess you could say that this summer at Planet Pom-Poms has helped me rediscover my true passions. And honestly, I haven't felt this good in years." Then she smiles her gazillion-dollar smile and hunches her shoulders up to her earlobes.

Clipboard girl pushes me into a corner behind one of the cameras and begins wrapping the microphone around my HoneyBees practice tee.

"So, would you say this is a second chapter for you?" I hear Coach ask Cappie from behind one of the cameras.

"No, this is a brand-new adventure. But I'm having a blast."

"Great, Cappie. We're all done for now," Coach says, nodding at the camera guy before ushering her straight ahead and into the corner with me.

And then we're both looking right at each other. And I never would've imagined that staring into Cappie's eyes, the exact same eyes that always looked out for me, would feel so scary.

"Hi," she says, still not breaking the stare contest.

"Um, you were really good over there." I finally look away and point to the chair. "Really professional and stuff."

"Thanks," she says as they remove the clip-on microphone.

Coach motions for me to move in front of the camera. "We're ready for you, Magic. And we're on a tight schedule," Coach explains, pointing to the chair.

I rub my sweaty hands down my jeans and when I look back at Cappie, she's turning to walk away.

"Um, wait," I yell at the back of her head, ignoring Coach. "Can we talk?"

She turns around and exhales. And then she says, matter-of-fact, "Look, Magic, I'm sorry things aren't working out the way you wanted. And I want to let you know that—" She lowers her eyes to the floor. "Claire told me that her roommate left camp this morning because she got homesick."

"And what does that have to do with me?" I shift from side to side, never taking my eyes off her.

"Well...she asked me to move in with her."

I clasp my hands over my mouth. "Are you serious?"

"And I told her that I would," Cappie whispers, finally looking back up at me. "I cleared it with Coach already."

"But you're *my* roommate."

She glances at the Stumbles as they open the tent flap and beeline over to me.

"I'm sure one of them would love to be your new roommate." Then she turns to walk away, but stops to look over her shoulder. "I'm sorry, Magic," she says, pushing past the Stumbles as they rush to my side. "And Magic, break a leg today. I mean it."

And then I'm sitting in front of a green screen, alone with Coach and the camera, trying to figure out how to put words into sentences.

I sulk into my HoneyBees tee, thinking about Cappie's last words. *Break a leg?* What's a leg when my heart is already broken?

CHAPTER 20

At first, when I get back to my room later that night, I just stare at Cappie's empty bed and remember how she dangled her head over it and made ugly faces at me when I wouldn't tell her who I'd been with at the beach. Then I start to cry because she moved all her stuff out. And I can't stop crying—I don't even know *why*.

It's not like she didn't give me a heads-up that she was moving out and moving up. But the tears still don't stop. And after a few minutes of ugly crying, I realize that I don't have any tears left. So now I'm sitting on the floor in a sloppy ball dry-heaving.

"Maaa-gic!" LuLu's soft voice sings from behind my half-open door. "Can I come in?"

"Yeah, *can we* come in?" Winnie asks, rolling past Lu with Brooklyn behind her.

But before I can answer, the Stumbles are watching over me.

"Sorry, but we heard whimpers," Lu explains.

"And not checking on our girl wasn't an option," Brooklyn says.

"Where's Cappie's stuff?" Winnie asks, looking around the half-empty room.

"She's gone," I whimper-sulk. "Claire's roommate went home, so she asked Cappie to move in with her."

Brooklyn folds her arms over her chest. "So. She finally crossed over, I see."

"To the dark side," Winnie says, and makes spooky sounds. Then Brooklyn fake-stabs herself with her fist.

"It's okay, guys," I rally. "Despite being on the floor crying like a baby, I'm getting through it. Really."

"Well, you're a better person than me," Winnie says. "I'd be falling apart if my oldest friend since tricycles and Barbie dolls dumped me."

"Winnie!" Brooklyn scoffs. "Always so harsh."

"She's right, B." I shrug. "Fortune says that Cappie

has to go her own way. And I have to go mine. And I think she's right."

"Me too," LuLu says, nodding. "Older sisters know about stuff like this."

"So I guess now you need a roommate," Brooklyn says, her smile covering her whole face.

They all look at one another and then back at me.

"Or *three*!" Winnie sings.

Brooklyn rushes out the door and yells over her long side braid. "Be right back."

I don't dream of objecting; instead, I blow my nose and watch her rush away with Winnie and Lu following along in her shadow.

After a few minutes, they plod back into the room one by one, carrying tons of stuff in their arms. Before I can declare a Stumbles sleepover, there are three sleeping bags lined up on the floor in the middle of my room. And by the time they're done putting the finishing touches on the mini remodel, my room is now the official Stumbles headquarters.

We slip into our jammies and settle into the forts, blanket tents, and blanket pallets scattered around the floor or onto the mattresses pushed together to make one giant mattress even bigger than my dad's. And that's pretty big because he's the tallest dad I've ever met.

"I have the most brillz idea," LuLu says, rubbing her hands together. "How about we have a Stumbles pajama jam?"

"Seriously? I've never had a pajama jam before," I admit to them, shrugging my shoulders in the air. "What is it, exactly?"

"It's where we sleep over and have our own pajama party."

"I've never been invited to one of those before. Whenever Cappie and I had a sleepover, we mostly watched her favorite movie and then went to sleep."

"Not at my jams," Brooklyn peps. "We blast the music and dance our butts off."

"And we get fab, sometimes trying on outfits with full-on fashion shows," says Lu.

Winnie pops her fingers to really bring the point home. "And we do each other's makeup and we share secrets and scary stories, too."

LuLu cringes at us. "I hate that part. All the scary stories give me nightmares."

"Well, we don't have to do that tonight," I say, pretty glad that I'm not the only one who still has nightmares. "But everything else sounds like a good time!"

"I know the first thing we should do at our pajama

jam," Lu says, grabbing her phone and scrolling through YouTube makeup tutorials until she settles on one.

"I know, too," Brooklyn says, dancing in place.

"It's makeover time!" they all scream.

Winnie rolls up her sleeves. "And guess who's first in line?"

"Are you ready?" Brooklyn asks, not really asking, as she squares my shoulders. "For a Magic Makeover!"

I glance at my reflection in the mirror.

Winnie shakes her head while sucking her teeth. "After the week you've had, you definitely deserve it."

"I could totally use one," I say, and turn back around to see them giving great HoneyBee faces with matching jazz hands.

Brooklyn dangles a flat iron in my face, and LuLu waves a curling wand in the air. I look at Winnie, who tosses me a thumbs-up with one hand and grips a pink-and-green makeup box covered in stickers with the other.

I smush my hands over my mouth. "My very own glam squad! But first," I say, cranking the music to my Party Animal playlist and shaking my butt around the room, "we dance!"

And for the next hour, we geek out about everything girly at our very own pajama party.

"Okay." LuLu raises her hand in the air. "I'm in charge of makeup."

She gets up and fumbles through the makeup kit on Winnie's sleeping bag. She applies eye shadow, blush, and even some bronzer on my cheekbones just like Fortune does.

"Almost done," she says, dabbing my lips with pink gloss. "Okay, now you can look at my masterpiece," she announces, waving her hands around my face.

"Nice!" I exclaim, rushing to stand in front of the mirror. "I look like one of those models at the mall that hands out perfume samples!" And I can't stop primping in the mirror, mainly because the bluish eyeliner and mascara she applied to my lids make my eyes pop, but not like an over-caffeinated raccoon this time. Winnie made sure of that.

LuLu and Brooklyn take turns working on my thick, bushy hair. When I pull it out of the ponytail, it's tangled and dry. But by the time they're done using their glammy hands on me, my salon-worthy braids are cascading down my back into curls that are super fluffy and ca-yoot!

"You look beee-yond cool, if I do say so myself," Brooklyn brags.

"I can't believe this is me." I run my fingers down the perfect braids. "I want to keep these gorgeous for MidSummer."

"We'll tie them down with a scarf so they look fresh for the big day," Brooklyn declares.

"Your eyes are gorge," Lu says. "I didn't even know they were brown before. I thought they were black like mine."

"With neon-green flecks in them," Winnie adds.

I stand in front of the mirror and bulge my eyeballs out of their sockets. "Never noticed the green before."

Winnie and Brooklyn gasp-turn. "You didn't know that?"

"I guess I don't look at myself that closely. I've never thought there was really anything to see."

"Well, hello!" Winnie gushes, while the other girls huddle around me, twirling me in circles. And within seconds, we're all giggling together.

"Can you believe MidSummer is tomorrow?" Lu says, cleaning up the leftover shadow and blush from the dresser.

"These past two weeks flew by," Winnie says, putting her makeup kit away.

Lu shakes her head in disbelief. "And if we all do well, we might actually get one step closer to becoming HoneyBees."

"Yeah," Brooklyn says, finger-combing Winnie's red curls. "But we *all* better rock it tomorrow and snatch those cool fifty points so we can get to Finale together."

I pull out my score sheet. "We need to get at least ten points in each category."

"Stunts. Dance. Freestyle," Lu starts, counting on her fingers.

"Plus tumbling. And something called the X factor," I finish.

"I'm still not confident about the routine," Winnie admits in a whisper. "I can't land my turns. I want to do a two-wheel 360 but—"

"A what?" asks Lu.

"A two-wheel . . . it's my version of a pirouette. They're called two-wheel 360s at the skate park."

"You hang at the skate park?"

"It's my second home. My hero is a guy who calls himself Wheelz. He can do all the tricks. I study his YouTube more than my math equations."

"Ohhh," Lu says. "Way cool."

"Opposite of cool, because when I spin around, I always end up facing the wrong way."

"Lemme help you," Brooklyn says, stretching her legs and watching as Winnie demonstrates. "It seems like your biggest issue is that you spin on your wheels fast enough to get around, but you don't spot anything. You gotta keep your eyes on one thing until you land right back where you started."

Then Brooklyn moves the sleeping bags and mattresses to the side and demos a series of turns in slow motion. And each time she spins back around to the front, she points to the crack in the wall where she's focusing, even though she's still not pointing her toes or holding her arms in a ballerina pose.

"Your turn, Winn," Brooklyn encourages. "Try this crack in the wall." She crouches on the top bunk and presses her finger into the dented plaster. "This is what I used."

Winnie takes a long deep breath and we all move out of her way. She rocks her wheels back and forth and then she pulls on her right one and pushes with her left. When she spins into her momentum, her chair whips around. This time when she lands, her head is facing Brooklyn, but her chair isn't quite there.

But Brooklyn hops down from the bed and high-fives her anyway. "Almost perfect, Winn. Keep trying. Practice makes perfect."

LuLu blinks her big, round eyes slowly. "Will someone help me with my high kicks?"

"But your kicks are already so much better, Lu," Winnie tells her.

"It's just that I get so winded in the kick line. It's hard to keep them at nose level when I'm struggling to catch my breath."

"I know what helped me," I tell her. "The trick to that is bending your knees when both feet touch the ground. Get the power you need from the bend *before* the kick. And remember to point your toes," I say, grinning at the Stumbles. "Learned that little nugget from Brooklyn."

But Brooklyn grunts. "Even though I know it, I'm still working on it, too. The biggest challenge for me is making it look sleek instead of clumpy."

Brooklyn and LuLu line up in the center of the room and link arms. Then they high-kick to Winnie's count.

"And five, and six, and five-six-seven, and eight!"

"See," Brooklyn says, pushing Lu into a deep bend before each kick.

"Wow," Lu says appreciatively. "That really makes a difference. I was keeping my legs straight before."

"Yeah, you gotta cheat a little, especially for endurance. Otherwise, you'll be down for the count," Brooklyn explains.

Then for the next hour, we take turns blasting the music from our playlists and practicing the big routine, our kick line, and a few easy tumbling moves.

My room has never felt so alive and filled with energy. I can feel the good Stumbles vibes bouncing off the walls around me as we work together to get better.

"Looks like we're all starting to get the hang of this," LuLu says, completely out of breath.

I push my shoulders back and say proudly, "And I didn't even need my inhaler."

"That's real progress," Winnie says, reaching into her duffel and pulling out a bag of Flamin' Hot Cheetos. She takes a handful and then passes the bag around. "Why do you think you haven't needed it?"

I shrug. "I'm not totally sure. Before, a lot of times when I was practicing or got nervous, my heart would start to race and for some reason, I couldn't catch my breath. Now I'm always counting the steps in my head. I think that's really helped me stay calm."

Brooklyn nods and then she says, "Maybe I'll try breathing and counting too when I get nervous."

"I'm doing better at staying calm, too," says Lu, taking the Flamin' Hot Cheetos bag from Brooklyn and shoving her head inside. After she takes a good long whiff, she comes up for air and chomps down on a few. "I'm not thinking about my mom the whole time when we're doing our kick lines anymore. And I can eat Cheetos without feeling guilty. *Yum.*"

"You think about your mom during kick practice?" Winnie asks. "That's one I haven't heard before."

"I actually think about my mom when I'm dancing, too," Brooklyn says back to her.

"And I think about my Grammy Mae," I say.

"Seriously?" Winnie asks. "All I can think about is trying to make my accommodated moves look halfway as cool as Brooklyn's hip-hop groove."

"But, Winnie, when you do that move where you pop a wheelie and then you rock your chair from side to side and move forward on each wheel...that is *everything*," LuLu gushes.

"You like that? I call that trick 'a wheelie into a crabwalk.'"

"Uh...yeah!" Lu says. "No other team has that stunt. It's *sick*."

"Thanks, Lu." Winnie passes her the bag of Flamin' Hot Cheetos again. "Now, tell us why your mom keeps showing up in your thoughts."

Lu pops a few more of them into her mouth. "Whenever we start the kick line, my mind races around. I think about my legs, I think about my feet. Sometimes I even think about lunch! But then, no matter what, I end up thinking about her." She pauses and looks around, not sure if she should continue. We all nod at her, so she takes a breath and keeps going. "I know you guys think she's hard on me sometimes, but the truth is...I worry about her more than she probably worries about me." She takes another deep breath. "My dad left just before school ended for the summer."

"Where'd he go?" Winnie asks, smacking on her Cheetos.

"Winnie! Girl!" Brooklyn pipes up.

Winnie stops to ponder what LuLu said. "Ohhh. I get it," she says, nodding. "Is it the *D* word?"

LuLu nods. "Sometimes I hear her crying at night."

I reach out for her hand and squeeze it. "I wouldn't want my mom to cry either."

"She doesn't know I can hear her through the wall in my bedroom," Lu whispers into the air. "All I want is for her to be happy again."

"I know what you mean," Brooklyn says. "I want my mom to be happy, too...wherever she is." She looks at me, and I look back supportively. "She died earlier this year."

"Oh no!" LuLu gasps.

"B!" Winnie covers her mouth. "I'm so sorry. We didn't know."

Brooklyn turns to Winnie and smiles. "It's okay." Then she looks at each of us. "Being here has been the best thing to happen to me since she died."

"It's been a nice break for me, too," Lu whisper-sighs.

"Me three," Winnie agrees.

All of a sudden my mouth feels like it's full of cotton. So I pick up a water bottle and turn it upside down to guzzle. "Losing my Grammy Mae was hard for me, too. She was like an earth angel to me. But time helps, B, even though nothing is ever quite the same."

"Is that why you keep her pom-poms so close to you?" asks Lu.

I nod. "It might sound silly to you guys, but they make me feel seen, and I've always felt kind of invisible."

"That's not silly. It's like she's watching over you, right?" Brooklyn asks.

"They give me confidence in myself. And I've never really had that before."

"They really are special." Brooklyn's eyes go wide. "And maybe she really is here."

Brooklyn helps Winnie out of her chair and onto the floor beside us. Then she sidles next to LuLu and a big yellow pillow.

"Thanks, guys."

"And there's nothing wrong with having a lucky charm," Brooklyn says, tapping a thin gold bracelet on her wrist.

"Your mom's?" Winnie asks.

Brooklyn nods, and wipes away a few tears as they roll down her cheek.

We all lean forward and pull her in for a tight bear hug.

"I don't know what I would do without you guys," I mutter into the huddle.

And it's the truth. Somehow, when I wasn't looking, they stumbled into my life and settled in and now I barely remember a time before them.

CHAPTER 21

"Magic! Wake up! Today's the day!" I hear someone say. "It's MIDSUMMER!"

When I pry open my eyes, the Stumbles are standing in front of me. I grin and hop up from the mattress on the floor. "Who's ready for the biggest day of our cheer career—second to becoming HoneyBees, of course."

We spend the next thirty minutes getting ready before dashing out the door with our pom-poms. We're bolting across campus toward the Great Lawn, but when we get to the Daffodil Field, LuLu stops us to do a quick once-over. She dabs at my eye makeup and stretches out my braids before moving on to Winnie. Lu tightens the purple shoelaces she let Winnie borrow, and then fidgets with her bra strap under her tee.

"Oh, wait, I almost forgot," Lu says, reaching into her bag and taking out four packs of Skittles. She hands each of us one. "I'm so glad we found each other."

"Me too," I say. Fortune and Cappie were both right: Things are different now. But that's turning out to be perfectly okay.

"Stop being mushy. I'm not screwing up my makeup because of tears," Winnie says. "Or eating green Skittles."

That's when I spot the Poindexters in the sea of parentals mingling with the Planet Pom-Poms powers that be. Mom is talking to Coach, and Dad's juggling his fans, signing autographs, and taking pictures. The Great Lawn looks like a magical ballroom under a blanket of fluffy clouds. Tables are covered in white linen and decorated with crystal everything with a big stage that was built just for today's dance-off. The red curtains rustle in the wind.

It's everything Fortune said it would be—and more. We take off running into it all.

"Over here, Pooh!" Mom's arms fly around her head, motioning for me. Bone-crushing hugs and slobbery kisses fill the air. They shuffle me back and forth, smothering me in their very Poindextery excitement. Honestly, it's nice to be back in their arms. And dizzying.

"Look at my Pooh!" Mom says, twirling me around in my sneakers.

"Mom, stop! You're making a scene." I wince.

"You're looking so cute." She shakes my waist from side to side.

I stand on my tiptoes and whisper into her ear. "I've been practicing so hard and working out every night. I even cut back on my junk food—and ate broccoli. Well, once." I grab her hand and wrap it around my inhaler. "My breathing has been better, too."

"That's how wars are won," Dad says, fathering me. "One victory at a time."

Fortune rushes up to the table in a strappy one-piece romper and heels. "We're so proud of you, Sissy. I told you camp would be life-changing."

"Whoa! And would you look at those muscles." Dad wraps his humongous hand around my bicep. "Big guns," he says, and makes an imaginary gun with his hand and shoots it into the air. As if that wasn't bad enough, he blows out the pretend gun smoke from the tip of the finger. I immediately want to turn the other way and run.

"And I see you're using Grammy Mae's poms," Mom says, eyeing my hands.

"I can't imagine dancing without them." Then I hug

the Poindexters and admit, "I'm really glad to see you guys. I missed you."

Coach stops our lovefest when she taps on the microphone and says, "Will all the Bees buzz backstage now?" She officially starts the show with a warm HoneyBee welcome to the Planet's friends and family. And I'm instantly jittery.

Fortune winks at me. "Break a leg, Sissy."

"We're cheering for you!" Mom hyper-waves into the air and Fortune bends down to my ear. "Don't be nervous. Just give it all you've got."

I wink back at her and race off.

"So nice of you to join us, Poindexter!" Gia says as I round the corner backstage and land right in the middle of the KillerBees. Her Rapunzel hair hangs over her pointy shoulders and she flashes a killer smile.

"Yeah, *so* nice," Yves repeats like a parrot.

I spot Cappie stretching with Claire, just a few feet behind the Killers. On impulse, I wave at her. It's easy to forget that she's not Team Magic anymore.

"Awww, how sweet!" Yves hisses into my ear, just loud enough for everyone to hear. "Tragic misses her bestie."

"*Ex*-bestie," Gia corrects.

I try to ignore the KillerBees, and instead head over to Cappie to wish her luck, but the Killers block me. "Cappie!" I try again. And this time I'm sure she sees me. She looks up at me and our eyes lock for two Mississippis. Then she looks away. No wave. No smile. Nothing.

The Stumbles rush to my side as the KillerBees snort and then flit away.

I groan. The show hasn't even started. What else could go wrong? That's when I peek through the curtain and spot Dallas and his family as they sit down at the very front table. Right below the stage.

My palms go sticky and I start losing my grip on my pom-poms.

Coach's voice echoes around backstage. "...And our returning Honeys will sit this audition out and have their turn at Finale. The other prospective Bees will perform two eight-counts of freestyle that demonstrate their dance ability while their prerecorded videos play. You can check them out on either of the big screens next to the stage. After their video, they will be judged on a stunt of their choosing. Then the girls will perform the signature routine with their groups. The routine includes the HoneyBee chant as well as freestyle."

I'd been working on my toe touch into split for my stunt. I'd have to fake the split, but Brooklyn said with my adrenaline soaring, I might actually get my crotch to touch the hardwood. Just the thought of it makes me squirm uncomfortably.

"If they make the cut today," Coach continues, "in one week they will join last year's HoneyBees and compete at Finale."

I try to review the steps in my head. But I can't remember how the routine begins or my opening formation either. I shake my head and bang on my ears, trying to clear my foggy brain.

"Just breathe," Winnie says. "You're going to be fine." She shoves my poms into my face. "Grammy Mae is right here with you, remember?"

I look back and forth between the Stumbles. Brooklyn is on one side and Winnie and Lu are on the other. "Okay. You're right. I got this."

"Let's go, girls. All Bees backstage. It's time," Coach says. Then she introduces the judges' panel. "We have our football coach and two parents from the PTA, an eighth-grade teacher, and our HoneyBee Middle captains, Gia Carlyle and Yves Lopez. They'll be fulfilling their duties as captains by serving as judges."

Fan-fricking-tastic! I think, wearing a sour smile. Having the Killers evaluate my every move is the last thing I need right now.

On center stage, most of the MayBees have already been introduced before Claire's name is called. Her pep-tastic introduction video rolls and we all watch in silence while she crushes her freestyle.

"Hi, my name is Claire Humphrey." Her video is supercute, mainly because she looks like Dora the Explorer and she's in the middle of the Great Lawn doing back handsprings in the sunshine. "I'm twelve years old, and I've been dancing for a whole year. I'm originally from Atlanta and I'm proud to be a Georgia Peach. But now that I'm in Santa Monica, I want to be a HoneyBee beeeecause"—*giggle giggle*—"my southern values and spunky style will add pizzazz to this already über-fabulous squad." Cue her jazz hands.

The audience applauds while Claire performs her signature stunt: an obscene toe touch that catapults her little frame into outer space. Then she takes her bow and moves back in line to join her group.

Screams and cheers from the crowd make even my nerves nervous. I snap out of it when I hear, "I'm Capricorn Reese."

Cappie's introduction tape rolls last, and she appears onscreen doing somersaults. "I'm good at a lot of things," her voice-over is saying as she grooves around onstage. "And dancing is just one of them."

"She's so boss!" Brooklyn proclaims, while Cappie freestyles like a champion dancer. "Oh, I'm sorry," she says, and scrunches her face into a frown.

"It's okay. She really is," I admit. And the earsplitting roar of the crowd is just confirmation.

"I've been dancing since I was three." Her video continues playing. "I did TV for a while, and even had a part in a movie, but in the end, there's nothing like dancing."

I peer around the curtain just in time to catch her rock her stunt: She hits a triple pirouette and lands it with a kick split. The audience hops to their feet as Cappie stands up and takes her bow. Then the MayBees prep to perform their signature routine together.

Our group is up next. To say I'm terrified would be a joke. Even the backs of my knees are sweating. And who knew there were sweat glands back there?

I peek through the curtains again. I can't help myself. Dallas is right in front. I feel like if I reach out I can touch him. Now I can't move my feet—that is, until Coach gently shoves me forward. "You're up!" she says.

I look down at the paper pinned to my HoneyBees tee: number thirteen, the most unlucky number in the history of numbers. Perfect.

CHAPTER 22

I can do this. I can do this. I can do this.

"First up in our next group is number thirteen, Magic Poindexter."

My introduction music pipes in. I don't budge. *Oh no, what if I can't do this!*

I shuffle out there anyway. And now I'm staring into the audience and just watching everyone fidget. They're staring right back at me very uncomfortably. And then I'm just standing there—watching them watch me.

My eyes dart around the crowd to find the Poindexters. What if I let them down? What if none of this goes the way they planned?

Finally, Dad shoves his hand in the air to toss me a big thumbs-up.

Mom bites down on her lip and crinkles her brows. "You can do it, Pooh!" I hear her shout. Did she just do that? In front of the entire Planet Pom-Poms?

"Hi, I'm Magic Poindexter." My video starts rolling. I cringe when I hear my voice. "But you can call me Maggs, or Maggie. Not that anyone ever does, but...you can." I nervous-giggle into the microphone they clipped to my HoneyBees practice tee that day.

"Magic!" Brooklyn yells at me. She's in the wings pushing girls out of the way. "Do what I do." Then she starts dancing behind the curtain. I study her like she's a really hard math problem. Finally, the answer starts coming back to me and I mimic her to the faint sounds of the music playing in the video.

Then it all rushes back, and I remember my dance moves. First, I hit the four hip pops with my arms in a high V. I exhale and the relieved audience exhales with me.

Okay, now this is starting to feel familiar. And I have successfully put everyone out of their misery. My poms shimmer down my side and then I pas de bourrée and back spin into a piqué turn. But this time, my ankle is wobbly, and I end up stumbling out of it. Still, I don't give up. I try to recover but now I'm two counts late for the lunge into the chassé across the stage that I practiced at our pajama jam.

When I look at Gia, she mouths at me *Tragic Magic!* while Yves grabs her belly and they both giggle.

My eyes find the Poindexters in the crowd. They're still on the edge of their seats, crossing their fingers and glancing up at God. They've waited twelve whole years for this. And I'm supposed to be stepping into my destiny.

I can't let them down, I think when I glance at Grammy's poms.

The strands are flitting around in the air, like they've been waiting for me. I shut my eyes and squeeze the handles of the poms. *I know you're with me, Grammy Mae.*

And within seconds, the steps to the next sequence are crystal clear and I feel stronger than ever.

My feet take off, shuffling through the double down, on beat. It's a struggle to balance, but I'm finally hitting my mark. Then I launch into a leap and I feel like I'm flying above the hardwood. When I look down, I'm more than a few feet off the floor and I can hear the audience applaud. I tell myself to keep going and focus on the turns that are up next. I step onto my tiptoes and pull myself into a double pirouette and spin down the stage.

I spot the top of a bald head in the crowd and I finish my last pirouette at the edge of the stage. My toes are teetering over the hardwood and I'm trying to find my balance. That's when I glimpse the big screen to my right and see myself in high definition and supersized, doing cartwheels through the Daffodil Field.

I try to ignore the distraction and find my balance. I can't believe that the tables of onlookers are cheering for me. Mom is clapping her hands together like a crazed fan and Dad is stroking his beard and bobbing his head up and down in approval. And Fortune is swiping away a few tears. I know I've made the Poindexters proud.

I fall back into position and prep to end my freestyle with a cartwheel. Then I hear my voice on the video again.

"I'm twelve years old and—" The audio skips. I try to keep dancing to my background music, mainly because Coach force-fed us that the show must always go on, even if disaster strikes. The audio skips again. "—and I'm in love with Dallas Chase. And I'm in love with Dallas Chase. I'm—I'm—I'm in love with Dallas Chase." The audience gasps as Dallas drops his dinner roll.

I watch it hit the ground in . . . slow . . . motion . . .

"I've never been around a boy like him before. He

talks to me like I'm a real person. And he's interested in stuff about me, and not because of who my dad is or because he played basketball. He didn't even ask for his autograph."

I remember saying most of those words that night in my dorm room. I never said I was in love with Dallas Chase. Someone must've added that. I distinctly remember talking to Cappie after my workout session with Dallas on the beach that night under the stars. Now somehow my words are echoing out in front of everyone.

"And when he talks to me, he looks right into my eyes." I watch the footage of myself up there, unable to move. "Like he's really looking at *me*. Like this," I say, making goo-goo eyes at Barkley.

The KillerBees hyperventilate into a fit of giggles but the video just keeps going, my kissy face on the big screens only making them fall out of their seats while pointing and snorting back laughter.

I shake my head. Why hasn't anyone stopped the video? I glance at Coach, whose eyes have glazed over in horror. She drops her clipboard to the floor.

I eye the edge of the stage and try to plot a route to my dorm to pick up Barkley, and then run back to my quiet house on the corner in Santa Monica.

But when I look up, all I can see is Dallas bolting

from the table and disappearing into the Daffodil Field, leaving a lawn of confused onlookers in his dust.

And then my knees go wobbly, my head is heavy and foggy, and my entire Tragic Magic world fades to black.

CHAPTER 23

When I force my eyelids open, the bright glare of the EMT's ocular flashlight is beaming into my cornea. I cringe when the last fifteen minutes of my life rushes back to me.

"This is absolutely unacceptable!" I hear Dad say as I peek through one eye from the back of an ambulance. I glance past the EMT who is talking to Nurse Molly and I sigh. Fortune is sitting by my side and Dad is standing in front of Coach Cassidy at the back door. He's got that look on his face that means serious business. I know it well and try to avoid it at all costs.

"Yes, Mr. Poindexter, I agree," Coach says, gripping her

clipboard. "I'm going to do everything in my power to find out who was responsible for this little stunt. And I'm going to make it my priority to make sure they are penalized."

"That was more than a stunt and it *definitely* wasn't little," Mom pipes in. I can see her hand is pressed into her hip and her foot is tapping feverishly against the pavement. "My daughter is in the back of an ambulance on a stretcher being double-checked for a concussion."

I try to move my arms and that's when I realize that I'm strapped down to a hard cot.

"Why am I being held hostage?" I whisper to Fortune. She removes the straps from my wrist. "It was for your safety."

I massage my fingers over my forearms and nod at Dad. "What are they talking about?"

"It appears to me that your captains might have some idea of who is responsible," Mom says. "They seemed to get the biggest kick out of this."

Coach furrows her brow and nods. "Yes, it appears that way, Mr. and Mrs. Poindexter. But I'll need to speak with them and also get clear evidence to support such speculation. And you have my word that I will. And if I do find evidence, they will be immediately dismissed from the HoneyBees team."

"We wouldn't expect anything less," Mom says.

"We'll be expecting to hear from you, Coach. And soon," Dad warns, and then turns toward me in the ambulance.

"Pooh," Mom says from outside. "The nurse said the children's Motrin will help."

But will it cure the post-traumatic headache still banging around my brain? And what about the humiliation and embarrassment?

"Can I have my inhaler back? And, uh, why am I in an ambulance?"

Fortune takes the inhaler from Mom and passes it to me. "You fainted. They just needed to make sure you didn't have a concussion."

"Or worse, my face all over social media with video of me being made into an even bigger joke than before. A true Tragic Magic moment."

When we finally get back to my dorm room, I immediately start speed-packing. There's no way I'm staying at camp. I can't ever face *them* again. And by "them," I mean the KillerBees—and Cappie, even though I'm not ready to accept that truth.

"I know that's how you feel right now, Sissy," Fortune

says. "But you might feel differently once you calm down. Why don't you stop packing and take a minute to breathe?"

I turn to her, my eyes wide. "They set me up. The KillerBees. I know they did. Didn't you see how they were laughing at me while I was being terrorized onstage?" I say, tossing Barkley into the bag, too. "Now, Barkley and I are going back to Santa Monica with you guys. We can't face them. Not ever again." I feel a tear slide down my cheek.

"Coach is going to get to the bottom of it," Mom says, and starts unpacking all the stuff I just threw into my suitcase. Then she squares my shoulders. "And I agree with you; this has someone's fingerprints all over it. But Coach is right, she needs proof."

Dad nods and tries to explain. "We can't go around just accusing people of—"

"Of recording me and then plastering it all over Planet Pom-Poms during my big audition?!" My mind races right into confusion. *How could Cappie do this to me?*

"You and Barkley will weather this storm, and once Coach has the evidence, those girls will be expelled from the HoneyBee program."

"But don't you understand, Dad? We're in a crisis.

This is *epic*." I shake my head and think deeply. "Planning my escape route has to be our top priority."

Then I throw Grammy Mae's poms in the wastebasket beside my bed.

Mom shoots Fortune a look that screams HELP. But Fortune shrugs back in return. "I completely understand why she wants to get out of here! And why she probably doesn't believe in the power of Grammy Mae's poms anymore."

"Magic, sit. Please," Mom says, and pulls the poms from the trash. But I shake my head at her.

"Those aren't my lucky charms. I relied on them and look what happened." I start counting on my fingers. "Let's see, I've lost my best friend, I'm pretty sure Dallas blames me for everything, I've been completely humiliated in front of the whole camp, and I don't have a shot at making this team, even though I've been working my butt off for it."

"Magic!" Mom says, holding the poms in her hands. "These are supposed to encourage you, to remind you of Grammy Mae's love. They're not supposed to alter the course of your journey."

Dad takes the poms from Mom and shakes them around. "They're supposed to show you what's possible, Champ."

"Grammy Mae's poms are meant to remind you that you're special, just like her," Mom says. "You already have what it takes to make the team inside of you."

Dad rubs the top of my head. "And you're brave, just like her." He grabs my shoulders and looks me square in my eyes. "You have to face the challenge head-on because in life, Champ, there will be obstacles that you have to overcome, even when everything inside of you says turn the other way." And then he does that fatherly thing: He leans down and kisses me on the forehead.

I fall back on my bed and Mom places the poms on top of me. But I don't want any part of them anymore. After that MidSummer Massacre, I'm convinced that I'm better off without any special help from Grammy Mae's poms. So I push them under the pillow and turn my back on them. "Honestly, I don't feel like I have any more strength left to fight."

"You don't have to do it alone," Mom says. "I'm sure your new friends would want to be right by your side. And they're counting on you to finish the summer with them."

I sit up and peer at the Poindexters. "Wait, what?! They all made it to Finale? Winnie? And Lu and Brooklyn? All of them?"

"That's right," Mom says, nodding while wearing a

slick grin. "Because of the Distress Clause, Coach Cassidy announced that the remaining girls who were slated to audition *after* your 'incident of immense distress' have all automatically advanced."

I victory-grin. "The Distress Clause, huh?"

"It's a loophole Coach Cassidy managed to find after your father insisted that she take a closer look at the rules."

Fortune crosses her arms. "How were they all supposed to perform after that? That would be asking the impossible."

"So, what exactly does this mean for us?"

"It means that since you all were put through, well, distress," Mom starts.

"And because it was clearly outside of your control," Fortune adds.

"You four get to move forward and audition again at Finale," Dad finishes.

This is really good news. But what about the Killers? I *know* they set me up. I can feel it in my gut.

Now I just have to find out how. And now, with the Stumbles on my side, I don't feel like I'm in this by myself. With all of our unique gifts, I know we can put our heads together and get to the bottom of this!

CHAPTER 24

I look to my left and see LuLu in step with me. And to my right is Brooklyn with Winnie rolling by her side. We're on a serious Stumbles mission as we march right over to the Great Lawn for practice the next day. Our heads are high in the air and our shoulders are pushed all the way back. Fact: We won't be stopped.

"We have to talk to Coach," LuLu says, stomping her feet into the daffodils with each step she takes. "She'll kick Gia and Yves right off the team. I just know she will."

"The Killers aren't going to get away with this,"

Winnie agrees, then she stops. "Wait a minute. How did Gia and Yves get that video in the first place?" Then they all turn to me.

Brooklyn rubs her chin. "Magic? Who were you having that conversation with? That person has to be involved, too."

Winnie rolls her chair around me. "Magic? Tell us. Who else deserves to have their pom-poms burned?"

They all stop walking and watch me as I squirm around the daffodils. I want to tell them that I think Cappie is the culprit who gave the Killers the video of me. But then again, I don't necessarily want Cappie kicked out of camp. She seems truly excited about becoming a Honey-Bee, and I don't want to be the one to take that away from her. Yes, I am fully aware that she might have done something awful to me, but for some reason, I'm still torn.

I squish my face into a frown and finally admit, "Cappie."

"Say what now?" Brooklyn shoves her hand onto her hip.

"I knew it! I *knew* she couldn't be trusted!" Winnie rants.

"We were in our dorm room that night," I say. "She was recording me dancing right before we had that mortifying conversation."

"Then all you have to do is tell Coach," LuLu explains. "She'll believe you. Cappie will have to spill what happened after she gave the video to the Killers. She's the key to it all!"

"Case closed!" Brooklyn yells, pretending to hit an imaginary desk with an invisible gavel.

"Let's go!" Winnie says, rolling in front of us toward the Great Lawn. "I see Coach standing by the stage. Let's talk to her before she starts practice."

LuLu grabs one of my arms and Brooklyn grabs the other.

But just as we're approaching Coach Cassidy, Cappie makes a mad dash toward me.

"I need to talk to you," she says, her eyes flicking back and forth between me and Coach. "Like *now*. It's important."

Winnie sucks her front teeth and crosses her arms over her chest. "I just bet it is."

I turn away from Cappie and smile at the Stumbles. "It's cool, guys. I'm good."

"We'll be right here if she wants to pull any funny business," Winnie says.

When we're finally standing behind a tree, hidden from view, I say to Cappie, "It's pretty clear to me and to the StumbleBees that you took that video of me and gave it to the Killers. How could you do that to me?" My voice doesn't even waver, that's how angry I am.

Cappie watches my foot tap around in the grass. When she looks up at me, I see what I think are tears in her eyes. "That's not what happened, Magic. I swear! I would never try to hurt you like that."

"Then what happened, Cappie? Because from where I'm standing, that's the only explanation. You had the video on your phone and it ended up on the jumbo screens during my audition. How else did it get there if it wasn't you?"

"I never meant for it to go that far."

"But you're saying that you sent Gia and Yves our conversation? Our *private* conversation?!" I'm fuming now and holding back tears. But as soon as Cappie nods, the tears race down my face. This hurts more than when I fell off my first ten-speed bicycle and broke my leg. I'm pretty sure they don't have a cast for this kind of hurt.

"I'm *so* sorry, Magic," she says. "I was being dumb. As soon as I pressed SEND, I regretted it. You *have* to believe me. I even told them to delete it, but I guess they didn't. I wanted to warn you, but I didn't think they were going to do something like blast it at MidSummer! I didn't mean for any of this to happen to you. And I'm really sorry."

"But why did you send it to them in the first place? Why were you so mad at me?" I ask. "What did I ever do to you?"

She glances at the Stumbles, but doesn't say anything else.

"Cappie," I say. "If you had just given them a chance you'd have seen that they're *really* nice. And you didn't have a reason to be jealous!"

"It's just that...I'm the only person you ever wanted to be around before. And I didn't know how to handle you having new friends." She leans closer to me and then she says, "Please let me be the one to tell Coach."

I look over at the Stumbles, who haven't taken their eyes off either of us. As a matter of fact, I don't even think they've blinked. And neither has Cappie.

"I—I guess that's fine," I stammer, taking one more look at the girl who used to be my closest friend. "But the KillerBees need to pay for what they did. Thank you for saying sorry." And then it's all too much for me to handle, so I turn and walk away.

"So? What did Cappie say?" Winnie asks as I walk up to her and the other Stumbles.

"She admitted she sent the video to Gia and Yves," I tell them. "But she didn't know they were going to do anything with it."

"Do you believe her?" LuLu asks gently.

I nod. "Yeah." Then I turn to Winnie. "You were right about her being jealous of you guys." Then I nod at Coach Cassidy. "And Cappie wants to tell Coach herself."

"I'm not so sure that's a good idea," Winnie says. "I think we should just tell Coach ourselves."

I wring my hands. "But I don't exactly want her to get kicked off the team! She's so happy now that she's dancing again...."

"You're kidding, right?!" Winnie grouses. "After what she did to you?"

"I can totally see how you could feel that way, Magic," LuLu agrees. "I'd feel the same way if she'd been my bestie."

"Let's give her a chance to confess," Brooklyn says. "Besides, she's the one with all the evidence."

I glance over at Cappie, who isn't celebrating either. Instead, she's kicking at the grass underneath her shoes. Then she looks at Coach, who is walking right up to us.

"Magic," Coach says, bending down until she's at eye level with me. "I just wanted to check in with you and see how you're doing."

I glance at Cappie, then I fidget with the bottom of

my practice tee. "I'm okay. I mean, I've been better, but I'm hanging in there."

"Glad to hear that," she says, patting me on the shoulder. "I'm in your corner, just know that."

"Thanks, Coach," I say, and look at Cappie, but she doesn't say anything as Coach walks up to the stage to begin practice. I shake my head at Cappie, disappointed that she didn't dish the deets about what happened. But she just hangs her head and walks away.

"Congratulations, Bees!" Coach says into the microphone, before applauding from the stage that's somehow still standing after MidSummer Massacre. "You should all be very proud of yourselves. Out of all the girls at Planet Pom-Poms this summer, you're the chosen twenty-five who will be advancing to Finale."

Screams and cheers erupt from the Great Lawn. High kicks and pink-and-gold pom-poms fly through the air.

"But this isn't exactly a celebration," Coach Cassidy says to all the giddy girls in front of her. "And I'm seriously disappointed."

"You tell 'em, Coach," Brooklyn peps.

"I don't know who thought that sabotaging another prospective Bee was a good idea, but pulling that stunt with Magic Poindexter's audition was a clear violation of the HoneyBee code. We are not a team that engages in that sort of dishonorable behavior. And it makes me angry...and really sad." That's when Coach looks down at Gia and Yves. "I expect better out of my team than that. Rest assured that I will get to the bottom of this and everyone involved will be immediately dismissed from the HoneyBee program. And Magic, I want to extend a sincere apology on behalf of the HoneyBee hive. This is not how we support each other. You deserve your chance to shine just like everyone else."

I feel the eyes of all the WannaBees on me. I can't help but fidget with my fingers; they'd all seen me at my most vulnerable. Then when I look across the lawn at Cappie, she's watching me watch her. And today is the first time I've ever seen real sadness in her eyes.

"Magic, you will be given another chance to audition for a spot on the team at Finale along with all the girls who were supposed to follow you. That's Louise Chen, Winfrey Walsh, and Brooklyn Ace."

"Are you serious?!" Gia yelps.

"Very!" Coach exclaims back at her. "And when I'm not at practice or in the gym with you all, I'll be spending my time getting to the bottom of what happened."

"We know what you did this summer," LuLu warns under her breath, making dagger eyes at the KillerBees.

"They need to be taken down." Winnie pounds her fists into the arms of her chair.

Brooklyn nods. "Don't worry." She grabs my hand. When I look down at our fingers, I see that the other Stumbles are holding hands, too, and their eyes are all locked right on the KillerBees. "I have a plan."

CHAPTER 25

A tiny ball of sweat rolls over my lip. It's salty and warm and it makes me question my sanity. I still can't believe we're doing this.

Brooklyn must've heard my heart trying to escape from my chest. "Shhh." She snaps her finger behind her. "Nobody move."

It's two days after MidSummer and we all huddle around her as she tries to pick the lock on the door of Gia and Yves's dorm room. Winnie and Brooklyn both swore it was the only way to get the evidence we needed to pin MidSummer Massacre on the Killers. And since Finale is only a few days away, it's now or never.

Brooklyn turns the bobby pin around in the lock with one hand and lodges LuLu's mom's credit card in the tiny space between the lock and the door.

"Looks like somebody's done this before," Winnie says.

"Don't ask questions you don't want answers to." Brooklyn side-eyes Winnie.

I'd only seen something like this done once before on *Law & Order* one time when Mom let me sleep with her because I was having nightmares. But *Law & Order* had turned out to be way creepier than the imaginary two-headed monster living in my closet.

"Got it." Brooklyn swings the door open and flips on the lights. "We're in like Flynn. My skills are a little rusty, but it's all good."

"Who's Flynn?" LuLu asks.

"Good question." Brooklyn shrugs. "It's something my dad says every time he opens our front door."

"Stumbles, focus!" Winnie says, circling the room. "They could come back any minute."

The layout in their room is just like mine. Two bunk beds. Two closets. And two desks next to two dressers. But unlike my room, this was definitely an upgrade in the girl-tastic department. There's a nail table with color-coordinated polish. Bronzer. A three-tiered makeup bar. Self-tanner. And extensions in every micro shade of blond.

LuLu pads over to the nail polish in a trance. "She even has Glamour Puss by Eden." LuLu opens the purple bottle and breathes in deeply. "This has been on back order for, like, a *year*." Her eyes glaze over like mine do when I've eaten too many double-chocolate doughnuts.

"Put that down, Lu." Winnie wheels over to her and snatches it right out of her hand. "We're on the clock. You're supposed to be in position."

LuLu is still giggling when she knocks a small plastic container onto the floor. I shriek when the lid flies off and something slithers out of it. "Is that a snake?" LuLu's voice asks. We all back away, and then, on cue, we freeze. Our eyeballs scan the floor.

"No," Brooklyn says, bending over to look at the box.

"Whew," I exhale, and everyone else relaxes, too.

"It's two."

Everyone shrieks.

"Ohmahgawd!" I hop around the room like I'm riding a pogo stick, scratching at my arms, chicken-pox style.

"They won't hurt you," Brooklyn reassures me. "They're just pets. And they're usually safe in their terrarium." She points to the plastic container on the floor.

"Yeah, but—"

And before I can argue, she's holding both snakes by their heads and making kissy faces at them. I turn to run out of the room, but Winnie grabs the bottom of my sweatshirt and yanks me back into position.

"We're all in this together." She only loosens her grip once I stop hyperventilating. "Guys! We need to find evidence. Any evidence."

The Stumbles scatter and begin checking their assigned locations around the room. Brooklyn hits the bookcase. LuLu snakes her body under the bed. A few seconds later, she comes up empty, except for the dust balls resting on her neon pink I'M A GOOD GIRL fleece. She picks them off and then hits the closets.

I was assigned the wastebaskets, windowsills, and desks.

Gia and Yves are in a captains' meeting and, according to the itinerary on Coach Cassidy's clipboard, it's only scheduled to last thirty minutes. At this point, we've already used up twenty-six, so that leaves us with four. Four minutes to find evidence so I can redeem myself and get revenge on the Killers.

I turn the wastebasket upside down and sift through snot rags, torn papers, hair balls, and receipts. "I've got nothing."

"Me too," LuLu says, shrugging.

"Same." Winnie sighs.

"Okay, Stumbles," Brooklyn says, digging into her pocket. "Then it's time for plan B."

"What's plan B?" LuLu says, her eyes saucering.

Then Brooklyn pulls out a handful of tissues from her hoodie and a Ziploc bag with green leaves in it.

"What's that?" I ask, padding over to her.

"Poison ivy," she giggle-explains, and then belly laughs. We huddle around her as she eases one big leaf from the bag, careful not to touch it with her fingers. She folds the itchy plant into the tissue and heads for one of the beds. We watch her smear the poison ivy all over the sheets.

"Where'd you get this?" LuLu gulps.

"A bush behind the gym. I found it when I was looking for Magic one day. I'd recognize it anywhere after Scout camp."

"Sooo good," Winnie says, taking a tissue and baggie from her. Then LuLu pushes her to the other side of the room.

"Should we really be doing this?" LuLu questions us. But Winnie points to the pillowcase and laughs. "An eye for an eye."

"It'll be the itchiest night of their lives," Brooklyn boasts.

Winnie throws her a thumbs-up. "Genius!"

When Brooklyn finishes her smear mission, she fixes the bed and then turns to us to explain. "I hold the Prank Queen title in my family. I pulled this one on my cousin after he drew a mustache on my face after I fell asleep at Thanksgiving last year."

"I'll do the honors," I say to Winnie, taking the tissue with the poison ivy in it from her. I lean over the other bed and follow Winnie's fingertip as it guides me across and then down the pillowcase.

"The itching will last a few days, maybe longer," Brooklyn says, giggle-snorting.

"And they'll be covered in that chalky calamine lotion," LuLu says. "It happened to me two years ago when I was at fashion camp."

"Forty-five more seconds," Winnie announces, looking at her watch.

LuLu presses her ear against the door. "I don't think so." She wrings out her hands and cups them to the door. "I think I hear them coming."

"Okay, everyone scatter. Get into second position," Winnie orders, and rolls her chair to the closet. Brooklyn and Lu pick her up and help her inside. Then Brooklyn hops in with her.

LuLu grabs the chair and breaks it down. "I don't

want to get caught. I can't die this way." She shoves the flattened chair under the bed, scraping the hardwood floor with the handlebars, and then she climbs under with it.

I'm still standing in the middle of the room. Brooklyn peeks out from the closet and points to the trash that's still in the middle of the floor. "Clean that up."

"And get into second position," Winnie orders again. "And flip off the stupid lights."

I can hear LuLu whimpering softly under the bed. "It's okay, Lu," I say, and hand-sweep all the trash back into the wastebasket before crawling under the desk.

Someone turns the doorknob and jiggles it. That's when I hear Gia scoff and say to Yves, "How many times do I have to tell you to lock the door? This isn't the Palisades. We're living with real-life regulars here."

"I did lock it…" Her voice trails off. "I'm *sure* I locked it."

"The lights, Magic," Winnie whispers.

I speed-crawl to the wall, flip off the lights, and speed-crawl back under the desk before the door opens. I've only moved that fast to double down on a HoneyBee beat before.

Gia opens the door and flips on the lights. I can see her legs and feet when she walks into the room and flings

240

her HoneyBee duffel onto the bed. She stops directly in front of the nail table. Yves is inches behind her. I hold my breath as she scans her manicure bar.

"Where's my Glamour Puss polish?"

"How would I know?"

"It was right here, between my Crazy Cowgirl and Ratchet Rebel." She stomps her feet and the hair on my arms stands straight up. "Where is it, klepto?"

"I didn't touch it. Pinkie swear," Yves huffs, crossing her arms. "But where's my pom duffel?" She looks around the room. "Crud. I left it outside."

"Figures. You'd lose your extensions if they weren't glued to your head."

"I gotta go get my duff. You coming or not?" Yves heads for the door with Gia priss-walking behind her.

Gia flips the lights back off. "Lock the door this time."

"I hate when you're hormonal," Yves says, closing the door behind them. "You're a total monster."

CHAPTER 26

Click. Clank. Click-click-clank.

I roll over to the other side of the bed.

Click-clank.

I pry open my right eye.

Click-click-clank.

The clanks are coming from the window, so I peek out and, to my surprise, I see Dallas Chase standing below my window with half a handful of rocks.

My room is still silent, except for Brooklyn's snoring. But that comes and goes, so I wait for her to gargle air through her nose again until I can push the window open as quietly as I can.

He looks up at me and a power surge of mushy feelings rushes through my nervous system, making me... nervous. They start in my toes and sizzle up to the ends of my big, long braids.

"I need to talk to you," he whispers up at me.

The digital alarm clock reads 10:35 PM.

"It's past curfew," I whisper-mouth back at him. "You're going to get me in trouble." When he doesn't move, I say, "It's past your curfew, too."

He nibbles the edge of his lip and mutters, "I know."

Instead of being practical, law-abiding Magic, I hold up a finger at him and close the window. Tiptoeing through the room of human minefields isn't easy. LuLu is asleep in a bed, and Winnie and Brooklyn are nestled in pallets on the floor. All our clothes are still in a pile next to the closet, so I grab Brooklyn's BIG HAIR DON'T CARE lavender tee and my jogging pants. Then I shove my arms into a metallic purple denim jacket and wrap my neck with a matching purple infinity scarf, both hand-me-downs from the fabulous Fortune.

The coast is clear in the hallway when I peek out to check. Without thinking, I scurry down the stairs, looping the drawstring on my pants, and bolt out the back door.

"Can we walk and talk?" he whispers, when I don't move past the back door.

"I guess."

"Sorry about the rocks. And about waking you up—I mean, if you were sleeping."

I rub the sleep from my eyes. "I was."

He snaps his football jacket and then pulls off his Dodgers cap to rake his hand through his carefree hair. "I need to explain something. It's been on my mind for a while and I want to do it before your Finale, and before we all go our separate ways for the rest of the summer."

I suddenly have no idea where to look, so I decide to focus my eyes on the half curls sticking out from under his hat.

He takes a few steps, and when he does, I turn around and glance up at my dorm window. That's when I spy the Stumbles all peeking through the blinds. LuLu rests her head in her hands and sighs. Brooklyn and Winnie take turns making kissy faces on the glass. I shoo them away with my eyeballs and try not to laugh.

When I catch up to Dallas, we walk for a while, neither of us saying a word. Instead, we watch the daffodils sway in the night air as the moonlight shines down, right on their green arms. And when the breeze blows, they all dance together under the stars.

"You're really good at cheering and dancing now,"

Dallas finally says. "I saw you practicing. On the grass with your friends."

My friends.

I think about their kissy faces and grin. I never really had *friends* before. Just Cappie. And she would never press her lips against anybody's window.

"You kept practicing and you didn't give up. I'm proud of you."

I shrug-smile. "The Stumbles didn't really give me a choice. With them by my side, it always seemed like it was going to be okay."

"You're lucky to have friends like that." He glances at me, and if I'm not mistaken, his cheeks start to turn red. "It's really working for you."

Now I'm suddenly keenly aware of *all* of me. My feet. My arms. My breath. But instead of gushing over my progress like this moment deserves, I really want to ask him about Gia. So I do.

"What's up with you and Gia?"

He doesn't hesitate when he says, "There's nothing going on."

I can't stop the word-vom from happening, so I keep pressing. "Since when?"

"MidSummer. We stopped hanging out after that."

I can't help the surge of hope in my chest. "But I thought your status with her was...complicated. What happened?"

"You," he says, without blinking. Then he fidgets with his fingers like I usually do.

But this time I don't have to urge to fidget, too. Instead, I lean in and shrug and say, "I didn't know they were going to show that video. Honestly."

For a few seconds, he just stares at a rabbit in the distance. And then he says, "You forced me to think about some stuff. And nobody's ever really challenged me like that. And then when everything came out at your audition, you know, in front of everyone...well, I was embarrassed. So I ran away."

"I really am sorry you had to go through that. Those girls never should have played that video."

Then he half smiles. "I'm good now. My coach sat me down and talked with me and so did Logan and some of the other guys on the team. They told me there was nothing to be embarrassed about. And I had time to think about what's really important." He eyes my braids and smiles.

I blush. "Braided by Brooklyn."

"Looks good on you," he says, but then he doesn't utter another word for two forevers. Silently, I start counting, and before I get to fifteen, he finally dives back into the conversation. "You're really different from everyone else. You're honest. And funny. And I know you wouldn't hurt me. Not on purpose." He pauses. "And when I put myself in your shoes after MidSummer, I was pretty impressed that you stayed at camp to finish what you started. The fact that you stayed is part of the reason I didn't leave."

"You wanted to quit, too?" I ask, totally shocked and thrown off by this admission.

He nods. "But my coach challenged me to figure out what I was actually trying to run away from."

I shuffle my feet around, feeling a little sad. And then look directly at him and ask, "It was me, wasn't it?"

"At first that's what I thought, too. I figured that I was running because I didn't want to be teased or made fun of. And because I didn't want to be bullied again. But then I realized that I shouldn't run away from someone because they remind me of who I used to be."

I wait for him to explain further, but he doesn't. And I don't push. I always hate it when people try to push me to share my feelings. So instead, we hang around the daffodils in silence.

After a few minutes, he exhales like he just finished one of Mr. Bower's Friday exams. And he blurts out, "The truth is, I wasn't always the jock or the cool kid that everyone looked up to. I was clumsy and chubby and seriously awkward," he whispers. "And don't forget about the braces and *really* thick glasses."

"Wait a minute," I say, squinting my eyes as I try to picture this version of him. "A little awkward, maybe. But clumsy and chubby, too!"

"Uh-huh." He grins. "They called me dough boy at lunch every day. It was pretty humiliating."

And then things finally start to make sense. "So that's why you believed in me so much," I say, nodding. "Why you never laughed at me, not when I fell off the bus or when I threw up right in front of you!"

"And why I never gave up on you, too." He looks right into my eyes this time. "The truth is, I know that with the right training and a ton of practice...well, you'll be a superstar out there on the field cheering."

"Well, Dallas Chase, I'll tell you one thing I know for sure," I say, finally putting the last pieces of the puzzle together. "I think I would've really liked that chubby kid who wore the braces and glasses. I bet he was pretty nice."

"To be honest, I never felt like that boy was good enough. But I've learned a lot from you over the past few weeks. He was perfect, just the way he was."

And that's when I realize my cheeks are starting to burn from blushing so hard. "I'm glad I could teach you something, too."

"Oh, you've taught me a lot," he says, bending over to pluck one of the daffodils from the dirt. And then he hands it to me.

I pluck an even bigger flower and gift it right back to him. "I guess that makes us even."

We've both learned big lessons this summer. And I'm glad I had Dallas Chase—Boy Wonder—and the StumbleBees to help me. I wouldn't have had it any other way.

Dallas pulls one of the petals from the flower and says, "If I had one wish, it would be to go back and tell that boy something. I'd let him know that it's all going to be okay. And that even though there's always the potential for improvement, he's good enough just the way he is."

"I'm sure he'd appreciate hearing it," I say. "I know how much it's meant to me this summer."

That's when Dallas grabs my hand and holds it in his. He squeezes my fingers and I watch his eyebrows crease his forehead. "But most of all, I'd let him know that one day he's going to meet a girl who will teach him the truth about being cool."

I nod back at him, because that's what this whole summer has been about: learning to be cool with who you already are. And while it definitely took me a while to get there, hearing Dallas Chase tell me that he thinks

I'm cool is the best end to an already great day. I'm just glad that we both figured it out.

We turn to head back to the dorm, hand in hand, and I'm so content that I don't even bother to count the Mississippis. When we get closer, I look at him and say, "I'm glad you stayed at camp, too. But Dallas Chase, Boy Wonder, there's still one big mystery left to solve."

"I'll tell you anything, Magic Olive Poindexter."

"Where, exactly, are you from anyway?"

"Can I trust you?" he asks, rubbing his chin.

"Of course." Then I shove my finger in his face. "Pinkie swear."

And that's when he leans in close and whispers, "Oklahoma."

CHAPTER 27

A few days later, we're running around the track and I'm not out of breath. And I can't believe it.

"We're closing in on the MayBees," LuLu says as we finish our second warm-up lap around the Great Lawn.

"Magic, you've really picked up your pace," Coach says as I push past her right into my third lap. She's standing in her usual position, watching carefully with a whistle and her stopwatch. "I'm impressed! You're crushing this."

I glance over my shoulder and see LuLu and Winnie right behind me.

"C'mon. Let's finish this thing strong today. The

MayBees are only half a lap ahead of us. Last week they were a whole lap ahead!"

Brooklyn glances at the girls in front of us. "She's right. We're getting faster."

"Or they're getting slower," Winnie says, laughing, rocking back and forth on her back wheels. "Let's do it," Winnie says, motioning for us to pass the group of MayBees.

"Everybody take a deep breath!" Brooklyn picks up speed and then motors right past us. But we're all on her heels, and one by one, we pass them, leaving them in our rearview.

"Great job, girls!" Coach yells into her megaphone.

"She sees us!" LuLu hypes. "Did you guys hear that?"

"Whatevs," Gia says, interrupting my groove. She turns to jog backward and spews, "So what, you know how to run. Big deal."

The Stumbles hold back laughter when we see that Gia's arms and legs are covered in pink calamine lotion. And Yves has it smeared all over her face and down her neck.

We're all struggling to hold it together, but when Winnie says, "Now your arms and legs match your pink-and-gold practice unis," we all belt out a series of giggles and guffaws. I almost trip over myself.

"When are you going to just quit, Tragic Magic? You and your posse of misfits?"

"Oh, don't worry, we *never* plan on quitting," Brooklyn warns her. "We're coming for you next."

"I'll always be ahead of you," she says, and takes off running and scratching.

When Gia is out of earshot, Winnie grabs my tee and fumes. "When is Cappie going to talk to Coach? I can't take much more of them!"

I don't say anything, but I know Winnie is right.

"It needs to be today, Magic," I hear Brooklyn agree.

"Or else we're going to do it for her," Winnie snaps.

We finish our final lap around the lawn and my eyeballs dart across the sea of sweaty Bees until I spot Cappie. She's standing next to Claire and she doesn't look like her usual confident self.

Coach gathers herself on the big stage and checks her watch. "Honeys, let's run through our chant and then break it down for all the Bees. After that, we'll run through the signature routine."

A few seconds later, a spirited voice yells into the air. "Ready?!"

Then the Honeys respond, "Oooh-kay!"

Tabitha and Sammie speed-somersault through the grass in front of a triangular formation of pink-and-gold

Bees. A super flexible toe touch soars toward the sky and then twists into a pike. As the Honey descends back to the planet, two more girls are towering over us, executing perfect Herkies and twisty flips, sky-high in the air. That's when Gia looks over at the Stumbles and rolls her eyes as she yells the words to the signature chant.

> **From the East**
> **To the West**
> **The HoneyBees, we are the best.**

And, as usual, she hits every sharp motion with precision.

> **We're gonna B-E-A-T beat 'em**
> **B-U-S-T bust 'em**
> **Beat 'em, bust 'em**
> **That's our custom**
> **HoneyBees will readjust 'em.**

"It's so cool," Winnie peps as they power-flip through the grass, and then move through four transitions and level changes.

The Honeys get into formation for a stacked pyramid. A veteran Honey is hoisted to the top.

"I can just see myself being tossed toward the sky like that," Lu squeals. "And then holding my leg in the air, high above my head."

"You're already manifesting your dream," I say, turning to Lu. "My dad always says you have to put your dream into the Universe and affirm it. Now it's just a matter of time."

We turn to watch the girl lower her leg and then pop into a toe touch before pulling her legs together in the air. The bases catch her in a flawless cradle.

"Those of you who know the chant, join us," Coach instructs from the stage. And we do.

Be aggressive
B-E aggressive
B-E-A-G-G-R-E-S-S-I-V-E

Then Gia runs into the middle of the formation and cartwheels into a twisty flip, landing on her butt. Yves follows behind her. And they both shoot their arms into a high V.

T-A-K-E-D-O-W-N
HoneyBees, we want a takedown
HoneyBees, we wanna win!

When the HoneyBees take their final pose and shake their poms around their pink-and-gold hair bows, the Great Lawn explodes into cheers and squeals. Everyone except the Stumbles. We're all thinking the same thing. That the Killers shouldn't even be here. I look at Cappie, but she's watching the Killers, too, and she's not cheering them on either.

"Everyone in your groups," Coach says. "The Honeys will come around to lead you."

"Let's do this!" Brooklyn peps.

Tabitha stops in front of our group and rallies us. "Okay, girls." She shakes her poms in the air. "Let's get started." Then she leads us through the chant several times. When it's time for us to build the pyramid, LuLu raises her hand when Tabitha asks about the flyer.

"Magic and I will be the base," Brooklyn says, standing next to me.

"And I'll do one of the chair stunts I've been working on after Lu hits her toe touch," Winnie declares.

"Let's do it," I say as we take our positions. Then I pick up my practice poms and ready myself for the chant.

"Um, Magic." Brooklyn pauses. "Where are your Grammy Mae's poms?"

"These are just as good," I say to Brooklyn, trying to get

her to overlook the fact that what I once considered prized poms were now in my room still stashed under my pillow. To be honest, I didn't bring them with me because I was still so wired about MidSummer Massacre. They've been the opposite of lucky for me, and that's putting it lightly.

"But they're part of your legacy." She shakes her head. "I wish I had a legacy to keep alive."

LuLu hops up and down. "You're continuing something special and the poms are part of it all."

I don't know how to tell them that I actually threw the poms in the trash. But since Mom wasn't having that, they'd have to stay hidden under my pillow for now.

"Let's run the chant one more time," Tabitha says, breaking up our group chat.

Brooklyn and LuLu nod and then flip through the grass in front of Winnie and me. Then I bend my knees and power up for a slightly above average toe touch. But when I start to feel a little nervous, I decide not to even attempt the pike. Instead, I attempt a double turn and I spot and spin back to the front of our formation with precision.

"We see you, Magic!" Winnie yells, and I can't help but do a happy dance around her chair.

Brooklyn is up next. And she punches through the air

in a very above average toe touch while Lu hits the pike jump and lands it.

"I did it! I caught air that time," she pipes into our circle.

"Yeah, you did," Brooklyn says, and high-fives her. But when Tabitha clears her throat, we jump back in formation and belt out the words to the chant:

**From the East
To the West
The HoneyBees, we are the best.**

We clasp our hands together and form a tight triangle with Lu in front and Winnie in the middle. Then Lu back flips out of position and Winnie wheelies into hers. Then she rocks back and forth before spinning into a two-wheel 360 turn.

"Go Winnie!" we all scream. And when she switches direction, she hits the turn on the other side, too. Even Sammie bounces around wearing a half smile.

We don't lose focus as we continue chanting:

**From the East
To the West
The HoneyBees, we are the best.**

Coach stops in front of our group. "Looking good, girls. Those turns are nice and tight, Magic. And the flips are epic, Brooklyn. You've all improved so much." Then she turns to Winnie. "And I haven't seen you do that trick before."

"Just something I've been working on."

"I can tell," she says, walking away. "Keep it up!"

Brooklyn kicks her heels into the air. "That was super sick."

"Ew!" Gia switches her hips over to us and spits her water out. "What do you misfits think you're doing? That's nawt hawt!"

"No, G. Let them have their moment," Yves says, standing behind her with an unopened bottle of water. Gia motions for it and then Yves unscrews the top and places it in her hand. "They'll never be on the court with us. Like *never* ever. Them becoming Honeys is the biggest joke of the summer."

Gia gulps the water and swishes it around her mouth. Then she spits it out again, all over my shoe. "As if!" She huffs and storms away, Yves trailing behind her.

"Dude!" Brooklyn yells. "That girl just spit on you!"

I take off my shoe and roll it around in the grass. "It's time!" I growl.

"Like *now*!" Lu says, and we all turn to march toward

Coach. But when we get to the front of the stage where she's standing, Cappie is already there. And she's handing her phone over to Coach.

"See, this is where I sent her the video. And I know I should've told you sooner, but Gia and Yves said they were going to tell you themselves. They said they wanted to take responsibility. And I believed them."

"Cappie," Coach says, and exhales slowly. "While I appreciate your honesty, I am going to have to penalize you for taking part in this."

"I understand," Cappie says, tearing up right in front of us. "I'll go pack my bags and be ready to leave in the morning."

"Wait a minute. You're not the one responsible for the video playing at MidSummer, so I am not going to expel you from camp. But since you did take part in this scheme, I am going to take your points away. That means you can still compete tomorrow at Finale, but your points will start at zero. You'll have to score a perfect hundred to make the team." Coach looks over at where I'm standing with the Stumbles. "Does that seem fair to you, Magic?"

I nod. I look at the Stumbles and they nod, too. "Definitely," I say. "I think that's fair."

That's when Coach Cassidy turns and grabs the microphone. "Gia and Yves, I need to speak with you."

A hush rushes over the Bees, and Gia and Yves slink to the stage.

"I explained after MidSummer that there would be serious consequences for whoever was responsible for the prank pulled at MidSummer," Coach says to the Killers while the Stumbles listen in the near distance. "And I meant every word. That was not acceptable HoneyBee behavior. And it will not be tolerated." Then she clears her throat and winces at Gia and Yves. "I am very disappointed in you two."

That's when Gia and Yves whip their ponytails around and shoot me with eye-daggers.

"I don't know what got into you both. But this is beyond acceptable," Coach says, holding up the video on Cappie's phone. "What were you thinking?"

Gia starts fake-crying. She nudges Yves, who quickly does the same, but her tears actually seem real.

"It's too late for that," Coach says. "The message on this phone says it all. Cappie clearly sent you both the video and you rigged Magic's intro."

Gia pleads with Coach. "Let me explain! It's not what it looks like."

"Go to your dorm and wait for me. I'm going to place a very important call to your parents and have them pick you up tomorrow."

Gia's eyes go wide. "But what about Finale?" Her voice is so high that it almost pierces my eardrums.

"Let me make myself clear: The both of you will *not* be allowed to participate in Finale tomorrow."

"No. You can't do that," Gia says, stomping her feet and waving her hands in the air. Then she grabs Coach's elbow. "We're HoneyBee legends. This is *our* team."

"We built this team," Yves says, crossing her arms over her chest. "It belongs to us."

"That's part of the problem," Coach says, peeling Gia's fingers from her arm. "This isn't *your* team. We are all one unit and we work together to win. We never work against each other. And now, *you* are no longer part of this team. You are officially relieved of your captain duties. Both of you."

"But you can't—" Gia says as Coach crosses her arms. Then Gia turns to us. "You're dead!" She tornadoes past us, digging her fingernails into her skin trying to scratch her pink arms and legs even harder. "All of you: *dead*!"

"I'm really sorry you had to go through this, Magic," Coach says. "HoneyBees represent an honorable school, Valentine Middle, and I have high expectations of my championship squad. Now. Let's get back to work."

"Wow," Winnie says, watching the Killers disappear into the Daffodil Field. "I really enjoyed that."

"So did I," Lu says, surprised.

"They definitely had it coming." Brooklyn nods.

We form a tight circle and look at one another. Then we all exhale and say together, "Stumbles!"

I glance over to Cappie, who looks relieved and a little sad. She catches my eye before turning away to join her group. But in my heart, she'll always be a Stumble, too.

CHAPTER 28

Who are we?
Stumbles!
What do we do?
Win!
How do we do it?
Believe! Achieve! Succeed!

Brooklyn, Winnie, and LuLu are shaking their poms
in the air while I yell out the lead questions in our chant.
We made it up this morning in my dorm room while
we prepped for Finale. We had a glam session with hair,
makeup, and a last-minute StumbleBee practice.

There was no denying that we've come a long way since that first day at Planet Pom-Poms Cheer Camp.

We huddle together and yell out one final time, "Believe! Achieve! Succeed!"

"We got this, Stumbles!" Brooklyn peps as she grabs her poms and opens the door.

"I'm so nervous, but I'm excited, too," explains Lu. She races out the door, on Brooklyn's heels. "It's like the first day of school all over again."

Winnie twirls her strawberry curls into place and then rolls toward the door as she says, "It's time to go out there and show 'em what we've got. It's now or never."

"You guys go ahead. I'll catch up with you," I say. "I'll be just one more minute."

"You sure?" Winnie asks. And when I smile and nod at them, she smiles back. I flop down onto my bed as she closes the door behind her.

I can't believe I've been at Planet Pom-Poms for three weeks. I got off that banana bus with so much fear and uncertainty about my cheerleading legacy. But now I'll be stepping onto that Finale stage with my cheer career riding on this last performance.

I miss Grammy Mae more now than ever before. I'd give anything just to hear her tell me it's all going to be okay. I reach under the pillow and ease the poms out.

I hold them in my hands and squeeze the handles, closing my eyes tight. "I just wish you were here."

"But Magic, I am. I've never left your side." It's Grammy Mae's voice, and I'm not sure if I'm imagining it, because it feels so real. And when I open my eyes, I can see her, smiling sweetly, even though I know she's not there. "I'm with you always."

My heart swells and tears rush down my face. "Grammy Mae."

"I'm so proud of you, Magic. You're discovering who you really are: a true leader. A real friend. A fierce winner."

I swallow hard. "I'm scared, Grammy. What if I'm not good enough? Everything is riding on this audition, and what if I don't make the team?"

"There's no need to be afraid. You're perfect just the way you are."

The pom-poms are warm in my hands as I watch Grammy Mae fade away. I take a deep shuddering breath and then I pad over to the mirror and look at the girl with the round cheeks and the big fluffy curls. And I repeat the words aloud. "You are perfect... just the way you are."

The canary-yellow sun has turned a cool burnt orange and is making a runway through the middle of the Great Lawn by the time I catch up to the Stumbles backstage. There's a big crowd seated at round tables with fancy white linens around the stage, and parents, friends, and more than a few photographers are buzzing from table to table. The energy in the air is frantic.

The perky Poindexters are seated at the exact same table as a week ago on that awful night under the stars. Mom is in her same seat with those same colorful nails sparkling in the sun. And Dad is right beside her, signing autographs and taking pictures with other old guys. Fortune walks around the table to her seat next to Mom. She's dressed in a lemon-yellow minidress with spaghetti straps and nude stilettos.

"She's so cool." Brooklyn peeks under my armpit through the curtain at Fortune. Then she points to a table behind the Poindexters and says, "There's my Grandma Betty Jean and my dad, too."

"I'm so glad they're here for you," I say, turning to Brooklyn.

"Please take your seats. We'll be starting in a few minutes," Coach announces.

"I'm going to go say hi to everyone," I say, and rush toward the stairs at the edge of the stage.

267

"Wait for us!" the Stumbles yell.

I run down to greet the Poindexters with Brooklyn on my heels, while Winnie's wheels roll down the ramp next to us.

"You're going to be great today," Mom says after I smush through all the tables to get to her. "And remember, we only want you to do your best; we're already so proud of you, Pooh."

"Mommm! I told you...please don't call me Pooh in front of my friends." I nudge her in the ribs with a stern warning.

"But it's true." Fortune squeezes my cheek and then bends over to plant a kiss right on it. "You are *amazy*."

The Stumbles are all staring adoringly at Fortune with their mouths hanging open.

"And Grammy Mae would be proud, too," Dad says, ruffling my hair.

I pull Grammy Mae's poms from my duffel and turn to Mom. "I'm not afraid anymore. She deserves to be here with me. After all, she started this legacy."

Mom fights back tears and I scrunch my face into a frown. "Mommm, don't cry!"

"I'm not sad, Pooh. Just proud."

"And no matter what happens, you're already a winner to us, Champ," Dad adds.

I'm squirming around in my HoneyBees practice tee as the Stumbles all listen to my family gush over me. It's beyond embarrassing, so when the Stumbles dash off to give their families hugs and squeezes of love, I'm relieved.

After a few minutes, Coach Cassidy taps on the microphone, and the Great Lawn focuses on her.

"Excuse me," Coach says. "Can I have everyone's attention?" She shifts her weight around and switches the microphone from one hand to the other as she welcomes everyone to the Planet Pom-Poms Finale and introduces the panel of judges. She reads their names off her list: two parents and the Valentine Middle football and basketball coaches. "And last but not least, our one and only, Principal Pootie."

"That's my cue to skedaddle, Dad."

"This is your big moment," Fortune says, giving me a smooch on my cheek.

"And we're so proud of Coach Cassidy for handling Gia and Yves with a no-nonsense approach," Mom says, before turning to Dad.

"I wouldn't expect anything less," Dad says, nodding at Mom as the Stumbles race back to my table, grab my arm, and pull me into the Finale whirlwind.

"Is Coach okay up there?" Winnie asks. "She looks more nervous than we are."

"I'm sure she doesn't want a repeat of MidSummer," Brooklyn says to Winnie.

I shudder. *Neither do I.*

Brooklyn rubs my back. "Don't worry, Magic. We got you."

Seconds later, Coach announces the order of auditions, and we laser focus on every word she says. "The final twenty-five girls have been divided into three groups and will perform the HoneyBee signature routine and end with a few counts of freestyle that represents their unique dancing style. In that routine, they will showcase their dance ability as well as that special X factor that we're really looking for in this final stage of the auditions. They have all worked hard and I am extremely excited about all the progress they've made," Coach finishes. "In Group A we have the returning HoneyBees, in Group B, we have Capricorn Reese, Claire Humphrey..."

"See." Brooklyn nudges LuLu. "We've all made progress. She just said so. We don't need to be nervous."

"...And in Group C, we will have Winfrey Walsh, LuLu Chen, Brooklyn Ace, Magic Poindexter..."

Coach glances into the wings at the WannaBees and then turns back to the crowd of excited family and friends. "The girls will be judged primarily on their execution of the choreography. But we're also looking for that special spark. And we'll all know it when we see it. We are a competitive team, so we need girls who will take the Valentine Middle HoneyBees to the next level. But even more than that, we are a family and we want to add girls who will make our family stronger and better." Coach air-claps. "Now let's get this show started."

The stage is dark. Group A performs without a single kick, jump, or turn out of place. And after they take their bows, Group B lines up in formation. And they look like they're ready to win. The poppy music with the hard beat starts and the Bees hit the four hip pops with their arms in a high V. Their poms shimmer down their side right before they pas de bourrée into a back piqué turn. Their feet are in sync as they speed through the hip-hop double down and wrap their poms around their bodies. They punch the low Vs and half Ts with crisp, tight arms.

Brooklyn is in the wings dancing with them. "They're really crushing it!"

"We gotta make sure our arms are tight like that," says Winnie.

"And don't forget to give HoneyBee face," I say, never taking my eyes off Cappie. "You know, be excited and peppy and don't forget to smile."

I watch her glide into the chassé across the stage. She lunges into a jeté leap and then spins out of it, twirling effortlessly into the next sequence. She smiles at the crowd, pumping her poms to the front, then to the side, and then around her body before snaking into the last eight-counts of several punchy hip-hop dance moves. She was born to do this.

Brooklyn's mouth hangs open. "She's so boss."

Winnie sucks her teeth. "She's all right. Nothing special if you ask me."

"Winn, are you ever going to forgive her for what she did to Magic?" LuLu whispers.

"She'll have to earn my forgiveness," Winnie growls. "In the meantime, I'm keeping a close eye on her."

"We bet you are." Brooklyn giggle-snorts. "But I'll give her a chance. Telling Coach was brave, and after all, we all make mistakes."

It felt good to know that the Stumbles have my back. But I've already forgiven Cappie, even though I know our friendship will never be the same. It'll be something different, and that's totally okay.

"We're up next," Brooklyn says, nudging me in the side as Group B takes their bows.

The stage curtain blows in the wind as we line up right behind it. LuLu is biting her nails and we all wait for Coach to cue the music to the big routine. I can't help but bite mine, too.

Within seconds, the curtain rises, the music starts, and it's time for us to get down to business.

I look out over the anxious crowd. And they all look back at me. And I can't help but feel like they're staring. And after MidSummer Massacre, can you blame them?

A skinny guy with thick sideburns whispers something into the photographer's ear and he rushes to the edge of the stage with his camera. He changes the lens and focuses it directly on me. He's so close that if I tumbled the wrong way, I'd fall right on top of his bald head.

My eyeballs crowd-surf to the Poindexters' table. Mom's fingers are crossed, and she has a forced, almost terrified smile stuck to her face.

"Work it out, Magic!" Fortune yells over the music.

I cringe when Dad shoves his thumb in the air and mouths *I love you*. It's like they're trying to get points every time they embarrass me.

In the distance, I spot Dallas and Logan jogging toward the Great Lawn. And then, I can't see anything else. Boy Wonder looks unbothered and supercool in his khaki dress pants, crisp white button-up shirt, and red Converse. He smiles at me, and this time I don't hesitate to smile back. After all, we're real friends now, friends who keep each other's secrets.

My heart skips a beat. But then, something really cool happens: I actually remember the beginning of the routine. I hit the first eight-counts with ease and pas de bourrée straight into the second.

I feel the nervous energy of the audience finally shift, and, table by table, they sit back in their seats and let out a relieved sigh. The hardest part was the beginning, and now that it's behind me, I can let THE DANCE take over. My toes are pointed. My leg extensions are straight. And my turns and leap-jumps are landing just the way Coach taught us.

I know it's not perfect, but it's good enough for the Poindexters to jump to their feet and cheer me on. Fortune even dances a few of the moves from her seat.

"Go Magic!" Fortune screams when I break down the cheer-pop mini-combo at the halfway point. Almost perfectly.

I'm not sure what I'm feeling. Maybe pride. Maybe

excitement. Maybe the realization that I'm getting closer to stepping into my legacy.

That's when I pop my arms into a high V and feel wet droplets bounce off my forehead. I look up and see a red plastic bucket of water teetering on the edge of a wooden rafter just above the stage curtain. I nudge Winnie, who's next to me shaking her poms with sharp, crisp arms, too. I nod to the bucket.

Winnie glances up at it. Her eyes widen as she fights to keep her smile on her face and turns back to the audience. "I felt it dripping on me," she says under her breath. "Look! It's tied to a string."

I moonwalk toward the corner of the stage, trying to look like I'm still part of the routine, and inspect the string. It leads to a hole in the floor and travels somewhere underneath the stage where I'm convinced Gia and Yves are hiding. "I can't see where it goes," I whisper to Winnie and LuLu, who are both looking at me worriedly as they continue their spins.

"We have to do something," LuLu hisses. "Somebody's got it out for us. And I know who."

Brooklyn snakes toward me, but I nudge her back to her position in the formation. "You can't stop the routine. No matter what."

The Stumbles continue to dance on cue, but they

don't take their eyes off the bucket. And when I look out into the audience, they're all looking up, too, trying to figure out what's happening.

The bucket is swaying back and forth on the edge of the rafter and it's only a matter of seconds before it's going to splash all over the Stumbles and ruin our routine.

I squeeze the handles on Grammy Mae's poms and feel a surge of calm pass over me. Then my heart swells with something that feels familiar, and the only way I can describe it is love. The truth is, I've waited my whole life for my big shot at being part of the Valentine Middle School HoneyBees cheer team. But right now, I can't think of anything more important that making sure my new friends are given a fair chance.

In the moment, I know exactly what I'm supposed to do. It's what Grammy Mae would've wanted, and it's what I want, too.

I open my eyes and peer down at the pink-and-gold strands as they sparkle and dance around my hand.

Sometimes things are bigger than me, and this is one of those times.

"Just. Keep. Dancing!" I yell to the Stumbles. "I'll take care of this!"

"But Magic, you'll lose points," I hear LuLu say as she desperately tries to keep her pirouette on point.

I grin as I watch her and Winnie land their turns. "You guys are worth it."

I turn my focus to the wings of the stage, my eyes darting around for something, anything, to cut the string—a knife, a razor, I'd even settle for a toenail clipper. But I don't see anything, until I spy Cappie digging into a metal toolbox on top of a speaker.

She pulls out a pair of small scissors and slides them over to me on the floor. I try to keep dancing on the side, but at this point, I know I'm completely off beat, and I have absolutely no idea what steps I'm supposed to be rocking right now. But I keep moving anyway, free-styling down to the hardwood to grab the scissors.

That's when I reach out and cut the string. But the bucket is still teetering back and forth, and while I'm looking up at the rafter, watching the bucket with my mouth wide open, I feel a few droplets just before the entire bucket of water splatters right over my head.

And I'm *soaked*.

Cappie gasps, and so do the Stumbles, right along with the entire audience of onlookers. I take a deep breath, feeling the icy water drip down my face and soak into my HoneyBee tee.

But Coach drilled into our heads that the show must go on. And I'm not going to let a little water stop me.

I kick the bucket into the wings and start dancing anyway.

I glance at Cappie, who shoots me a thumbs-up as her look of shock turns to relief. It's almost like we're *The Magic Capricorn Show* all over again, but new and improved.

By the end of the last sequence, Coach Cassidy is standing in the wings, looking up where the bucket of water was, and then back at me. She scribbles something on her clipboard and then nods at the judges, just as the song comes to an end.

I study the crowd and see the Poindexters wiping away what look like tears. And they're not the only ones caught in this monumental moment. A few tables away, LuLu's mom is standing on her feet cheering for her daughter and Lu couldn't be any more thrilled. Brooklyn's dad and grandmother are at the same table yelling their hearts out. They look so happy, but I know Brooklyn would give anything to have her mom here.

Everyone is so proud of us. And I'm feeling proud, too, when I look at Winnie, who mouths *Thank you* at me. And all I can do is smile back at her because I know I've learned the biggest lesson today—my fears don't define me, but my courage does.

The Stumbles are all in perfect formation when I cartwheel into a deep split right into the middle of the stage, with my toes pointed and my poms shaking in a high V—for an epic, although wet, StumbleBees Victory.

CHAPTER 29

The energy backstage is out of this world. The prospective Bees buzz around me, taking turns drying me off as we all wait with anticipation to see if our summer dreams are about to come true.

"Magic, I can't believe you did that," LuLu says, jumping up and down as she squeezes the leftover water from my hair.

Brooklyn throws her arm around me, and Winnie tugs on my arm and says, "You put your dream on the line for us."

"I couldn't let you guys go down for a dumb KillerBee

prank," I say. I'm still giddy from the performance, and the thought of Gia and Yves doesn't knock me down from this pedestal—even as I shake out the remaining water from the bottom of my HoneyBees tee. "We're all in this together!"

"Stumbles!" they say, high-fiving me and covering me in love. And I know I made the right decision. Being there for them was the least I could do after they've been by my side these past three weeks.

Coach Cassidy walks onto the stage and says, "Can I have all the HoneyBee candidates to the side of the stage?" Then she shuffles the papers in her hands together. The Stumbles and I all look at one another, crossing our fingers and offering up one last prayer.

"It looks like we've reached that time of this very... *interesting* Finale," Coach says as my heart pumps high-octane blood through my veins. My hands are sweaty and my legs are limp from all the kicking and leaping. I glance down at Grammy's poms and I smile, because no matter what, I'd still do it all over again.

Coach looks at all the Bees in the wings. "This is always my favorite time of summer camp at Planet Pom-Poms." Coach tries not to get emotional as she fumbles through all the judges' score sheets.

I peek around the curtain and see the Poindexters point back at me before crossing their fingers in the air. There was nothing more for me to do. Bottom line: I gave it my all, despite the KillerBees' attempt to sabotage the Stumbles' chances of winning.

Coach's eyes scan the WannaBees in the wings. They stop on me. "Now it is with great pleasure that we announce your new HoneyBees for the Valentine Middle Cheerleading Squad! If I don't call your name, we appreciate all your hard work this summer and wish you nothing but the best. And remember, we never count anyone out—there's always next year."

Coach rattles her papers and then announces into the air, "Claire Humphrey."

Claire happy-wriggles through the huddle of Bees in the wings as Coach continues reading off her master list of lucky ducks. I see Cappie jumping up and down, shouting out congratulations.

I can hardly stand still, I'm so nervous. Brooklyn grabs LuLu's hand while Winnie holds on to her other arm, and Lu reaches for my fingers. I squeeze them tight, not even worrying if my palms are sweaty.

"Capricorn Reese," Coach says, before going to the next name on the list. My heart pounds when Cappie eases past us to take her place on the stage. "Good luck, Magic," she whispers as she passes me by.

"Thanks!" I yell back at her.

"Louise Chen," Coach's voice bellows into the microphone.

We all turn to Lu, ready to jump up and down and scream in excitement for her. But LuLu's eyes are closed and all of her fingernails are wedged between her teeth.

"Lou*ise* Chen," Coach says again, emphasizing the syllables.

"That's you!" Brooklyn finally yelps, fist-bumping a clueless Lu.

"Me?" LuLu gulps, looking around our circle. "I made it?"

When Brooklyn pushes her onto the stage, LuLu turns back to us and I spy real tears in her eyes.

"Rielle Turner," Coach continues as LuLu runs to her spot. "Brooklyn Ace."

Winnie tugs at Brooklyn's wrist. "And that's YOU!"

Brooklyn firecrackers into the air and then aerial flips her way onstage.

"Did you know she could do that?" Winnie gasps.

I clap my hands together so hard they start to burn. "Nothing she does surprises me anymore."

Winnie bobs her head at me and states with certainty, "She deserves it so much. We *all* do."

When Coach moves down the list, my breathing gets spastic. Winnie looks like she's deep in prayer, so I grab her hand and she half smiles back at me.

That's when Coach says, "And Winfrey Walsh."

The crowd jumps to their feet and howls in excitement for her. Winnie rolls out and they all fan-roar. As she takes her place in formation, one by one, it seems like the entire planet stands up and cheers.

I'm beyond thrilled for the Stumbles, but I've been counting. And now with only twenty slots open and eighteen girls already crowned, I'm feeling like my destiny might not be as close as I thought. I peek around the curtains again. Fortune is counting the Bees onstage and Mom and Dad are both staring at the curtains, waiting to get a glimpse of me.

But when Coach says "Marlo Rivers" I don't have an ounce of hope left. There's only one spot remaining.

I look around at the handful of WannaBees waiting in the wings with me. And as Marlo skips past us, they don't look like they've got much hope left either.

"And last but not least..." Coach eyes her master list.

I look down at Grammy Mae's poms and close my eyes. *I know you're with me, Grammy Mae.*

"Magic. Olive. Poindexter."

My HoneyBees tee suddenly feels too tight. I can't feel my toes. I look out at the stage where all the Stumbles are waving at me to join them, their grins wide and their eyes shining.

Coach smiles at me in the wings. "I saw something today that made me think the HoneyBees need a little Magic on our team. She sacrificed her audition for her group mates. And that is exactly what our HoneyBee family is all about. Not only was her audition competitive, but she put it all on the line to make sure her team didn't stumble or miss a beat. And for that, I'm honored to offer her a spot on our new squad. Magic, come take your place with your new teammates."

"Ma-gic! Ma-GIC! *MA-GIC!*"

When I hear the crowd chanting my name, I forget all about my frozen feet and run out to take my place beside Marlo, who smiles and moves over so I can be next to Winnie.

"Congratulations, girls!" Coach says before turning to the crowd. "Parents, families, friends—please join me in welcoming our newest Valentine Middle Cheerleading Squad!" Coach exhales into her Beedazzled HoneyBees tee while the new squad fires off our cheer tricks into the air.

The Stumbles rush over to me and we all squeeze each other tightly.

"We did it!" Brooklyn yells, stopping to moonwalk around us.

LuLu jumps up and down and shakes her poms in the air. "We're total HoneyBees!"

"Now," Coach says, matter-of-fact, "friends and family, please join me in doing the honors. Let's give it up for our new team as they perform the HoneyBee signature routine together for the first time."

But it doesn't hit me that we made it until Coach cues the music and motions for the new squad to begin the dance. And we *are* the new squad!

The Stumbles fall right into formation and within seconds, we're all caught in a HoneyBee dance trance. The crowd is on their feet rocking out with us. I beam when I see Fortune marking the moves in her seat and Mom getting in on it, too. I confidently pas de bourrée into a high kick and my leg flies high above my head, almost touching my nose.

The Poindexters wave their arms in the air and yell out my name.

"Ma-gic!"

When I turn around to my new teammates, they're following my lead and finishing the routine with some sick freestyle. I smile, watching LuLu two-step into her chest pop, shooting her pom-poms into a high V. Brooklyn back handsprings across the stage, and Winnie wheelies, then rocks herself into a perfect one-wheel 360. On the last four beats, I leap through the air and tumble into a front tuck roll and land in a jaw-dropping Chinese split, right in the middle of the stage just as the music stops.

The Poindexters are chanting my name.

"Ma-gic!"

"MA-GIC!"

That's when I see Dallas still teetering on the edge of his seat, so I shoot my arms into a high V and smile down at him. I marvel at the pom-poms sparkling in the air. I'd be willing to bet that Grammy had something like this in mind when she gave me my unique name.

With the crowd on their feet and a real Planet Pom-Poms celebration in full effect, my friends topple me, smothering me with hugs and giggles.

When the curtains close, we shuffle down the stairs and head toward our families' tables, but Coach stops us before we can get there. I mega-grin at her when she says, "Thank you for all that you did today, Magic. I don't know what we would've done without you."

"It was the right thing to do, Coach. The Stumbles deserved a chance just like everyone else."

"You girls have really come a long way," Coach says. "And I'm very proud of you."

Coach reaches down to give us all hugs and that's when I spot them running toward a bush behind one of the tables on the lawn: the KillerBees!

I tug on Coach's jacket and point to Gia and Yves. "They were the ones who planted the bucket!"

"Don't you worry," she says. "That's already being handled."

And boy was she right. My eyes go wide when I see Principal Pootie stalk over to the bush where they're hiding. His finger is waving around in the air and his head is shaking from side to side. And to top it all off, their parents are right on his heels.

The Stumbles and I all high-five one another, doubling over in laughter.

"Congratulations," Dallas says, appearing beside me as Coach Cassidy walks away toward the bushes. "I *knew* you could do it. You were amazing up there."

I stare straight into his dreamy green eyes and say, "Hi." But before I can think of what to say next, the Stumbles don't waste any time making googly eyes and kissy-face sounds behind us. "Thanks...for everything."

"No prob," he says, grinning. Then he nods and says, matter-of-fact, "You should come to Logan's birthday party next Saturday." Then he turns to the Stumbles, who immediately stop gushing at us. "And bring your friends. I can text you the details."

I can't hold back the mega-blush that's turning my face a solid Crayola red. "Yeah. Sure. I mean…" I look over at Fortune, who's walking up to us. I smile even harder when she winks at me. "That sounds fun."

"Cool!" And then he takes off to join his family. But when he turns back around, he says, "See you later, Magic Olive Poindexter." And I feel my feet and legs almost go limp. It's official: I definitely have a crush on Dallas Chase!

"I hate to interrupt," Mom says, but she probably doesn't. She waltzes up to us as Dallas leaves and I'm feeling even lighter than I did five minutes ago. The Stumbles all make googly eyes after him and don't stop until Mom stretches her arms around the Stumbles. "You girls did an amazing job today."

I stand on my tiptoes and turn to Fortune to whisper-ask, "Did Boy Wonder just invite *me* to a birthday party?"

"Why wouldn't he have?" She pinches my cheek. "And I'll take you and the girls shopping for it."

LuLu, Winnie, and Brooklyn are still in awe, talking about our upcoming shopping trip as they rush off to their families.

"You were pretty great up there, Champ," Dad says, bringing me back down to earth. "And I've never been prouder."

Mom leans in and pats me down with a linen napkin.

"I'm all dry now, Mom."

"That whole stage could've gotten wet and ruined your friends' routines, let alone caused injuries. But you sacrificed yourself and got drenched," she fusses. "Pooh, you saved the day!"

"And you proved that you have lots of special gifts," Dad adds. "Just like your Grammy Mae."

I'm feeling more like a Poindexter than ever before when Mom reaches for my hand. "And now you've stepped into your legacy." She points to Grammy Mae's poms. "Pull the streamers back." And when I do, Grammy's initials aren't there anymore.

Instead, that same golden glow is swirling around the initials MOP.

Mom struggles to fight back tears. "The journey is yours now." Then she looks at the Stumbles in the distance. "And you've got the perfect friends to join you on it."

I stare at my initials and realize I'm fighting back tears, too.

"C'mon, Magic!" the Stumbles yell after finishing

their lovefests with their support squads. They wave me over as they skip toward the Daffodil Field. But Fortune taps me on the shoulder and nods at a table in the distance. I turn around and see Cappie standing there. Watching me.

Then she smiles. And I smile back. But she doesn't walk away this time; instead, she starts our Reptile handshake...and I finish it. We both wave goodbye.

And that's perfectly okay.

The Poindexters smother me in hugs and kisses before I dash off to catch up with the Stumbles, running toward this new chapter in my life.

The orange sky is glowing, casting shadows against the mountains while the daffodils wave in the dusk breeze. LuLu squeals when she cartwheels through the air, and when Brooklyn joins her, the heads of the summery flowers swallow their arms. I run past them and somersault into the lazy evening sun while Winnie spins around us all. Nothing but soulful, sweet laughter echoes above us. I pluck a flower and leap through the rows of daffodils, living out my dream with my new best friends.

Everything is exactly how it's supposed to be as we giggle under the fading sunshine.

I look into the distance at the empty stage and I'm sure that the best is yet to come. I fold the poms into my chest and thank Grammy Mae for choosing me. And when the Stumbles' laughter fills the air again, I thank her for them, too.

I know now that my life will never be the same, because today is the day that I, a former Tragic, made true Magic happen.

ACKNOWLEDGMENTS

This book wouldn't be an actual thing if it weren't for Timothy Shannon Johnson. Thank you for everything that is you, and especially for believing in my sparkly dreams.

I have the most fab team of editors on the planet. A victorious thank-you to Lisa Yoskowitz and Hannah Milton. Thank you, Lisa, for your rock star vision, your ability to see the potential of what would one day become our very special story. Hannah, you are my brilliant shero, whose superpower involves sprinkling barrels of pixie dust all over my words—and also compassionately talking me off the ledge! This book is as much yours as mine. I'm beyond honored to know you.

There's no doubt that I'm the luckiest creative to have the phenom that is Marcy Posner as my agent and editor, and also my chosen family. You're everything I dreamed but never knew I deserved. You continue to make me better. Thank you for the gift of hope, for believing in me and all my little stories, and for waving your wand in my direction. I will love you infinitely with my entire heart.

To my dear friends and family, IRL and online, thank you for your unwavering support and for, quite frankly, saving my life.

And lastly, but MOST importantly, thank you, Blondie (read: Mom) for loving all of me—and for letting me sleep in your guest room. Cheers!

Timothy S. Johnson

ERIKA J. KENDRICK

is a national speaker, mental health advocate, and former NBA cheerleader. She is a Stanford University graduate with an MBA in marketing and international business from the University of Illinois. *Squad Goals* is her first middle-grade novel.